CHAMPION OF
THE WORLD

BERNARD DUNNE was born and raised in Neilstown, west Dublin, the place he still calls home. The son of Olympic boxer Brendan Dunne, he competed in his first boxing match at six years old, and spent the next twenty-three years training and perfecting his craft. Narrowly missing out on qualifying for the 2000 Olympics, Bernard went on to a hugely successful professional career, with twenty-eight wins from thirty fights. He finally beat Ricardo Cordoba in a dramatic eleventh-round knockout at the Point Depot in Dublin in 2009 to become super-bantamweight World Champion. Since retiring from boxing, Bernard has written two books and several television series, worked with the Dublin Gaelic football team and as a sports analyst on RTÉ television, and become the High-Performance Director of Irish Boxing. Bernard lives in Dublin with his wife Pamela and their two children, Caoimhe and Finnian.

BERNARD DUNNE

CHAMPION OF THE WORLD

THE O'BRIEN PRESS
DUBLIN

First published 2019 by
The O'Brien Press Ltd,
12 Terenure Road East, Rathgar,
Dublin 6, D06 HD27 Ireland.
Tel: +353 1 4923333; Fax: +353 1 4922777
E-mail: books@obrien.ie.
Website: www.obrien.ie.
The O'Brien Press is a member of Publishing Ireland

ISBN: 978-1-84717-977-7

Printed in the UK by Clays Ltd, Elcograf S.p.A.
The paper in this book is produced using pulp from managed forests.

Contents

Chapter 1

The Neilstown Boy

There are two things I get slagged about when I'm talking to people or just walking around. The first is a fella called Kiko. I'll talk about him later. The second is where I'm from. When I tell people I'm from Neilstown, they usually say, 'Oh, where's my wallet?' or, 'I'm glad I left the car at home tonight!' If you believed everything you heard, or read in the papers, you'd think the place where I grew up was a war zone, a dangerous, horrible place to live.

Actually, it was quite the opposite. I always loved the place, and I still do. Most people who have grown up there feel exactly the same way. Neilstown moulded me. It made me who I am today. I probably spend as much time there now as I ever did.

My parents moved to Neilstown in 1978, when my older brother, William, was two. I was born there, on 6 February 1980, and our house on Neilstown Avenue would be my home for the next twenty-one years. Next door lived the Jennings family, and Paddy, who was born two months before me, became my best mate from when we were tiny. He still is today, though we don't get to see each other as often as we used to.

Neilstown has always been one of those places where neighbours were actually neighbours. They cared about each other, and looked out for each other. When someone needed a hand with anything, the neighbours would all pitch in. In much of the world, we seem to have moved away from that sort of spirit, towards a more closed-off life. I like the Neilstown way, with great neighbours who you can depend on.

Growing up was pretty different back then to how it is now. We didn't have all of the amazing technology that children have now. We had a football and a few marbles, and in September we had conkers. Ah, good old conkers! You would sit them in the freezer for a couple of days, trying to harden them up, to make them as strong and unbreakable as possible, before bringing them out to battle. The thing about playing conkers was, it was as dangerous for your knuckles as it was for the conkers! Not the ideal pastime to have if you were hoping to become a world boxing champion ...

Myself and Paddy Jennings, or Redser as he was usually known, were like Tweedledum and Tweedledee. Where you saw one, you would always see the other. We were always up to something, but never really anything too bad. We never hurt anyone – well, apart from ourselves, that is.

One day, as we were out and about, looking for something to do, we spotted a man tying his horse and cart up to a tree at the back of our houses. Now, being the bright sparks that we were, we decided that we would become horse rustlers and take a free ride on the poor animal. Looking around to check that no one was watching, Paddy leaped up onto the cart, while I untied the horse. Just as Paddy gave it the first 'Yup!', your man who owned the horse appeared, back from the shops.

'Here, you two little gurriers!' he roared at us.

'Jaysus, Paddy, wait for me,' I said. 'Give me a hand up before we get caught.'

Little did I know, the rope that had been around the tree, keeping the horse where the man had left it, was caught around my foot. As we were making our getaway, it tripped me up, and I fell flat on my back in front of the horse. The beast was kind enough to jump over me rather than trample on me, but unfortunately the cart was not as thoughtful. The two wheels of one side of it rumbled straight over my legs, and I let out a yelp. Paddy jumped off, and ran to get Mammy Dunne. That was the end of our horse-rustling days, as well as the end of me being able to walk for a couple of weeks.

Now, speaking of bright sparks: Myself and Redser were out collecting bees in jam jars one fine day, and we wandered down a lane around the corner from our houses. It had big bushes in it, and we reckoned we could capture a couple of big bumblers or red-arses in there. As we were hunting our prey, I heard a loud buzzing sound coming from a pole in the lane. The cover was off it, so I went for a nose around. I couldn't see anything inside, but it was making one hell of a buzzing sound. I called Redser over, thinking we'd hit the bee jackpot. Redser watched, while I stuck my hand in, expecting to catch the mother lode of bees.

In that moment, Bernard Dunne was in serious danger of being no more. The buzzing sound that we were hearing wasn't a huge swarm of bees. It was live wires in the electricity pole making the noise. Grabbing them wasn't the greatest moment of my life. I got an electric shock that nearly threw me out of my shoes.

Once again, Redser dashed over to my house, yelling for Mammy Dunne. She ran around, to find me stretched out on the ground. The ambulance was called and off I went, not for the first time, to Our Lady's Hospital. In fact, at this stage, the hospital staff must have been wondering if anyone was ever watching what I was at – I had been in when I was very young and I fell and fractured my skull; then there was the horse-and-cart incident; then, to top things off, another time I had been bouncing on the bed and fell off, hitting the corner of the wall and cracking my forehead. There was blood everywhere that time. By now, my folks were on first-name terms with the doctors and nurses!

Anyway, on this occasion when we got to the hospital, the doctor told my parents how lucky I was to be alive. Apparently, if it had been raining, or if I hadn't been wearing my cheap, ninja-like pump runners, I could have been a goner. No more little Bernard! But thankfully it wasn't, and I was, and so I am still here. After an examination and a couple of tests, I was left in the care of a junior doctor. The skin on my hands had become a little melted and soft, so he wrapped them up carefully in long bandages. We thanked him for all his help, and off we went home.

A couple of days later, we had to return to the hospital for a check-up, and to get the bandages removed from my hands. The melted skin I told you about? Well, when that fantastic junior doctor bandaged my hands, he should have bandaged my fingers separately. Instead he bandaged them all together as one, and the skin became webbed together between my fingers. I was now like Donald bloody Duck! After the new doctor sliced the skin to separate my fingers, I could have given our old helpful friend a dig, but I had to sit and get bandaged all over again.

Those little scraps and scrapes are all part of growing up, I suppose. And all of these little accidents cannot ruin my fond memories of Neilstown. It was, is and always will be my home. Even when I was travelling all over the world, I couldn't wait to get home to my friends and family. Great people. The homecoming parties they would have when I came back with a medal! Food, drink and music, and the whole street would be involved. It was fantastic.

When I turned professional and left for America, I always kept in touch. A couple of the gang from the street even came over to watch me fight in Las Vegas. The Neilstown crowd on tour, waving flags and singing songs. They were great support, though maybe not the greatest of singers! And even when the dark days came, and they did come, the Neilstown people always stood by me. I will never forget their support, and when and if I can ever repay it, I will. They don't build too many neighbourhoods like that anymore.

Chapter 2

Why Boxing?

According to the Oxford Dictionary, boxing is 'the sport or practice of fighting with the fists, especially with padded gloves in a roped square ring'.

What this doesn't mention is the focus that boxing demands, the mental strength needed to push yourself to the limits. Being hit in the face isn't something that you grow to enjoy, but it's certainly something you grow to accept. It's funny, but it's something that I actually miss about my sport. It makes you feel alive.

When you step into a boxing ring, whether as an eleven-year-old going in to his first fight or a thirty-year-old getting ready to compete for a world title, you experience the same feelings. That tingle in your belly. A mix of nerves, excitement and even a little fear. But then, when that first punch lands upon you and you feel the crack of leather against your skin, you quickly forget about that tingle and a razor-sharp focus takes over.

It is like nothing else matters, nothing except that person who is standing in front of you, trying to land that winning blow. I have often thought, why would someone put themselves through this? Now that I am on the outside, looking in, I know why. Nothing else can give you that absolute clarity, that feeling of being alive, truly alive. The laser-like focus on just exactly now – not thinking about the bad day you had yesterday, or the homework that you don't have done for tomorrow – that feeling is amazing.

Boxing for me was a natural – or more than that, an inevitable – road for me to travel. With my Dad coaching my two older brothers, and having been a boxer himself, it was a choice of either boxing or move to another family. Luckily, I discovered that I really liked the sport. I also discovered a natural ability that probably surprised most people who saw me – this little, cheeky-looking kid who you could barely see behind the gloves and headguard once they were on.

Inside that boxing ring, once the bell went, that little angelic-looking kid would change into something fearsome. 'Jaysus, Brendan, where did you find him?' my Dad would be asked when they saw the devastation I would wreak on my opponent.

Neilstown Avenue had plenty of kids around the same age. There were the five Jennings boys, three Drumms, two Kellys, two Baileys, the Dunne clan and plenty of others. It was a fairly new estate, filling up mostly with people moving out from the inner city. Like most young boys growing up there, I very quickly learned how to look after myself.

With so many young lads living on the road, there was always something to do. Rain, hail, sleet or snow, we would always be outside, getting stuck into a game of poles, heads and volleys or knockout. We would start a friendly game of football, but inevitably, someone would question a goal, or accuse someone of a foul, or someone just wanted to moan because they were being beaten. Remember, we had no goal-line technology back then. Then there would be some name-calling and pushing, and then a couple of punches if someone was really in a bad mood. I was generally off-limits. Not because I was tiny, but because my two older brothers, both of whom were boxers, were always around.

William and Edward were my protectors. William is the eldest, five years older than me. Then comes Eddie, who is not my biological brother but my cousin. His parents both died when he was young. We all played together, so if you messed with one, you messed with us all. This gave me the confidence to go in for the tackle, to go for the big shot at goal – more confidence than I should have had, as I knew my brothers would have my back. When they got older, they eventually got fed up with me tagging along with them everywhere they went, but for now, they enjoyed it as much as I did.

Sport was a big part of life in Neilstown, especially on the Avenue. Neilstown Rangers was a big football club, and Neilstown Boxing Club was about 300 metres from my house. It was only a short stroll away from my house, so you might be surprised to know that I never ventured through its doors. No, I would box for CIE Boxing Club in Inchicore. And so would nearly every male who grew up on the Avenue.

You see, my Dad, Brendan Dunne, an Olympic boxer in his day, was coaching in CIE, and he brought all the boys down with him. With Clondalkin growing so quickly, and with plenty of young lads running around, my Dad knew that he had the perfect environment for breeding boxers. There wasn't much to do in the area, very little in the way of activities or facilities to keep young people occupied, so there was also a real danger of young guys and gals being led astray through sheer boredom.

But my Dad always knew that boxing is much more than just a way to fill your time. It develops self-confidence – not that the cocky young Dunne needed much more! For me, boxing was so much more than just an opportunity to terrorise kids who jumped into the ring with me.

When you train as a boxer, you know that you are able to defend yourself. And in learning the discipline of following instructions in the gym, you also learn that you can complete tasks all by yourself.

When I was growing up, boxing was popular mostly in working-class or disadvantaged areas. Through boxing, young kids in these areas learned that focus, hard work and dedication can lead to success. And it gave these kids, with their limitless energy, a chance to release that energy in a safe environment, while keeping out of trouble.

Growing up in boxing provided me, and every young athlete who walked into our gym, with positive role models. Here were guys who had been there and done it before we did, guys who would sit down and talk to us about their experiences. They would tell us how boxing had given them the chance to travel abroad, when for most people in those days, the nearest they would get to going away on holiday would be a trip to Butlin's for a weekend.

This focus and discipline, and learning to follow the instructions of the coaches, didn't only benefit us in the gym.

It also helped most of us with our school work. It taught us how to listen, and how to complete tasks that had been set for us. The hard work that we would put into our boxing was mirrored in our school work, as our coaches would link the two together – bad reports in school would lead to no training. Peter Perry and my Dad, the CIE Club's two main coaches, said they wanted boxers who could 'think inside the ring'. 'Boxing is not just about the big guy wins,' they would tell us. It was about being able to 'outsmart your opponent'. Being a bit of a shortarse myself, definitely not the big guy, I was always quite pleased to hear things like this from the coaches.

Many parents don't encourage their children to try boxing, imagining that it's just like getting into a fight in the street. But there is so much more to boxing than just swinging your fists and hoping that you hit your opponent more than they hit you. Boxing teaches many powerful life lessons, like how to deal with defeat, the importance of respecting others and respecting yourself, and ultimately that without hard work you will not get to where you want to go.

In neighbourhoods like Neilstown, boxing also had a huge social purpose. It gave kids like myself, full of energy and mischief, an outlet for that energy and a direction and focus in life.

When I was growing up, all of the boys from the Avenue participated at some point in CIE. Every one of those young boys grew up to be successful in their adult life – whether in terms of a career, a good family life with kids or becoming champion of the world. They all grew into fine people. Now, I am not saying that boxing was the only factor that made those kids develop as they did. But growing up where we grew up, it surely helped. All sports can have this effect, but where I grew up, we did not have a huge choice of sports to pick from.

I have had many friends who were not as fortunate as us. Some got involved in crime and drugs, and some of these unfortunately are not with us anymore, while others have been locked up. Some found their way out of it eventually, and have been able to move on.

Sport has fantastic power to create change. Once you realise that it is not just about winning or picking up a trophy, you can have so much fun and learn so much about yourself and about life. Sport can help to give kids direction, and teach them new skills – how to focus, how to work as an individual and as part of a team. It also teaches the hard lessons – that sometimes setbacks happen, sometimes things just don't work out. It was a big part of what kept all the boys from the Avenue out of trouble.

Getting involved in sport from a young age, whether team sports or individual sports like boxing, encourages good habits that remain with you for life. It can surely also help with the obesity crisis that now faces the world. When you look at all of the values and skills that sport can teach children, it makes you wonder why we don't focus more on this type of education in schools, rather than just all the academic work.

Chapter 3

Rasher Enters the Boxing World

It was Friday afternoon, and myself and Paddy were walking home from school. We stopped off at the shop to pick up some sweets. We got money every Friday to get something nice after school. We lived about 200 yards from the school, so even for a pair of six-year-olds, it was hard to get lost on our way home.

After picking up our ten-penny bag of jellies and a package of onion rings, we walked under the pylon and cut across the dump. 'The dump' was the name we gave to the field behind our houses. It was where our annual bonfire was set up. We obviously weren't the brightest of kids – we would pile up whatever bits of wood we could find, and basically anything else we could get our hands on, into a great heap, and then set it alight right under large electricity cables! The dump was also the venue for football matches against our rival areas.

On our way across that day, we spotted my Grandad's car, parked outside my house. Today was fight day. We were travelling to Drogheda, and I was going to have my first fight!

Yep, that's right, at six years of age I was about to step inside a ring and fight for the first time. In reality, I had been in the ring all my life. Before I was born, my dad had boxed in the 1976 Olympic Games, in Montreal, Canada. He was the first ever light-flyweight champion of Ireland. And then there were my two older brothers, who boxed in the club where my dad trained, CIE Boxing Club in Inchicore. Like any little brother, I was a pest to them and followed them everywhere, and this led me to taking up boxing properly at the age of five.

To be honest, I was too small to do most things at the club. I had to stand on a chair to reach the punch bags and the floor-to-ceiling ball. The gloves were nearly as big as me, but that never stopped me. Once I got inside that ring, I was like a different person. I loved it.

Okay, I spent most of my time in the club messing around, but when I stepped inside that boxing ring, and they put that big, sweaty, smelly headguard on me, which I could barely see out of, and those gloves that looked like I was wearing two big pillows on my hands, I was no longer that innocent-looking child. I instantly turned into a little Tasmanian devil, ready to take on all comers whatever their size or age.

I look back now and wonder what the hell my Dad was thinking when he first brought me down to the club and let me into the ring. I now have two children myself – Caoimhe, who is ten, and Finnian, who is nine – and there is no way that their mammy would let me bring them into a boxing ring to slug it out with kids bigger and older than them. But I do know exactly what my Dad and everyone else there was thinking when they saw what I was doing with kids twice my size. This kid can fight! And they were right. And on that day thirty years ago, when I was getting ready to travel to Drogheda, I was thinking that the rest of the world was about to see the same thing.

Grandad had arrived very early that day. It was only two o'clock, and we weren't due to leave until around 4.30pm. But he was more excited than anyone. He used to come down to every training session to watch me do my thing. He loved it. I would sleep in his house every weekend, and at Sunday morning Mass, before we went to training, he would be telling anyone and everyone about his grandson who was going to be a world champion boxer. You can only imagine what they thought when they found out he was talking about the little knee-high kid standing behind him!

That was the routine that I had as a kid. I'd finish school on a Friday, go training down in CIE, and then home to Grandad's house, to stay there for the weekend. I'd go up the park to play football and mess around in the playground, or I would hang around the zoo, not far from my Grandad's house. Then, on Sunday mornings, it was off to Mass at nine o'clock, then home for breakfast, which was always eggs in a cup with bread soldiers for dipping, made by my aunt Betty, who would have it all timed perfectly so that it'd be waiting for me when I walked in. Then down to Peter Perry, my coach, for training in CIE – 'the slaughter house', as Grandad liked to call it.

Anyway, on that Friday, we arrived in Drogheda around 7pm. The journey seemed to take no time at all, with four of us crammed into the back of the car, laughing and pushing and shoving. It was great preparation for my first ever fight.

We all headed inside. A big crowd had travelled up from our club, as we had a few guys fighting on the bill. Dad and Peter talked to the Drogheda coach, Christy McKenna, and they started matching the fighters up. 'Yeah, they're about the same size, let them fight,' 'No, he has too many fights for him, that won't work,' and so on, until they got to me.

'Have you got anyone for little Rasher to get in with?' was the question. Yes, that's right, 'Rasher'. That was my nickname. To be honest, I don't remember why I got that name. Maybe it was because I was so small and thin, but anyway, that's what they called me.

'Jaysus, how old is he?' came the reply.

'He's six, but he'll be grand with any lad a little older than him. He's Brendan's son.' My Dad being Brendan Dunne, a former national senior champion and Irish Olympian, got me some kudos, so Christy McKenna said, 'Okay, we have a lad. He's ten, but we'll get him to go easy in there.'

Go easy? The bloody cheek. I'll show them go easy, I thought.

Peter Perry was forever telling me to go easy, but what he really meant was, *Go get him, Bernard.* CIE Boxing Club was beside St Michael's estate flats in Inchicore. There were plenty of young lads around there who were rough and tough, and quite a few of them fancied themselves as boxers. They would come around to the club looking to join, but then do nothing but mess and stop other people from training. The order would then come down from Peter: 'Rasher, get your gloves on.' When there were new lads messing around in the club, this only meant one thing: Peter didn't want them staying in the club, and it was my job to convince them that they didn't want to come back.

Gloves and headguard on, and it was showtime. I would go at them like a little Jack Russell at a chew toy. I was relentless. All the while, Peter would be shouting, 'Take it easy, for God's sake, will you?' Sparring over, a couple of bloody noses and a few tears shed, and that was the last we would see of those lads.

We went to our changing room that evening in Drogheda, to get the shorts and vest on. My vest had to be sellotaped at the back, as it was falling off me it was that big. Some shadow boxing and a little bit of punch pads with my Dad, and I was ready to go.

My fight was the first thing on the bill. We walked to the ring. A cloud of smoke filled the gym – this was 1986, and back then there was no ban and no common sense when it came to smoking around people who were about to get into a ring to fight. Thankfully, being as small as I was, my head had no chance of being up in the smoke clouds! Last instructions from Dad and Peter were: 'Just box behind the jab, and you will see the openings.'

'Come on Rasher!' came the cheer from the Dublin crowd as I entered the ring. *Ding ding!* and out I go. Popping that jab, just like I had been taught. This kid I was against was in for a surprise. He saw this little six-year-old, who he was a whole lot bigger and stronger than, and I'm sure he was very happy about that. But this was my chance to shine, and I was about to change his happiness and confidence into shock and fear. I loved boxing, especially fighting. I was technically very good. I could outbox most people that I was put in a ring with, but my problem often was that I loved to fight. Maybe it was because I was so small that I felt I really needed to show my opponents who was the boss.

So it's double jab, then I danced around the ring a little.

Another jab straight into his face and then *bang!* I followed it with a big left hook. The hall went silent for a second, and then I just remember my name being called out: 'Rasher! Rasher! Rasher!' Now a look of fear had come over my opponent's face.

I was swarming relentlessly all over him. Throwing punches from all angles – straight jabs, right hands, left hooks, uppercuts from either hand. I was on fire. The more the crowd cheered, the more I was trying to do to please them. *Ding ding ding!* Three rounds done, and I was the winner. Six years of age, but I felt like a champion already.

'Jaysus, Peter, what are you feeding them down there?' asked Christy. 'He will be some fighter by the time he is eleven.' Eleven is the age when you are allowed to properly fight. I had another five years before I could get in that ring for real, but when I did, oh man, those eleven-year-olds would be in for a shock!

Grandad was proud as punch. He did nothing but talk about it all the way home. Straight into Ma he went, and he told her the whole fight, blow by blow. He may have exaggerated some parts just a little. At one stage, I think he had me fighting three guys. He couldn't wait until Sunday Mass.

Chapter 4

Learning My Trade

Technically, for my age I was very good. My problem though was that when they realised that trying to box with me was getting them nowhere, I was all too happy to engage in a war with my opponent. If they were brave enough to throw the gauntlet down and go for an all-out attack, I was only too happy to oblige. This would annoy my Dad, and drive Peter crazy – he would often be the one to hit me hardest in a fight.

I would come back to the corner after a round, thinking, 'Yeah, I'm on top here,' after beating my opponent up for two minutes. Maybe I had even knocked him down with one of the many blows I had been raining down on him.

In the corner, I'd be met with a 'sit down there', and a little slap across the face. Peter would be going nuts that I was not sticking to the plan. I was fighting with this guy, giving him plenty of chances to hit me. He wasn't hitting me, but that wasn't the point. Peter and my Dad would have laid out instructions for me before the fight, all about making it as easy as possible for me. They would always be trying to get me to stick to the old boxing principles: 'Hit and don't get hit.'

It was now 1992. I was eleven years old, and boxing in my first National Championships, at 31kg. I had already won the League Championships, and I had followed that with a County Dublin title, which qualified me for the Nationals. I had stopped my opponents in the quarter-final and semi-final stages, and was now chomping at the bit to get in there and do the same in the final. The last six years of training and hard work had all been leading up to this.

I despatched my opponent in the final, just like I had in the previous rounds, and I was crowned the Boy 1 National Champion at 31kg. Felix Jones, who was then president of the Irish Athletic Boxing Association, sent me off with a little rub on the head and a 'well done, son'.

The show was on the road now, and I was keen to keep learning and driving in the right direction. For my second year, and the Boy 2 Championships, you can literally just copy-and-paste from year one.

My first major challenge came as a Boy 3, when I came up against a fellow two-times National Champion – Robert O'Connor, from the Sunnyside Boxing Club in Cork. He was a tall, rangy southpaw, a left-hander, who liked to box at range and pick his opponents off. We were in the opposite sides of the draw in our weight category, and we both dominated our opposition up to the final.

The day came for the fight, and there was a lot of talk of this being 'the big test' for me. People said that O'Connor just had too much reach and height over me, that he would be able to just keep me off with his long-range shots. In our warm-up in the dressing room, Dad and Peter were telling me to get as close as I could, to stay in close to his chest and let my shots go from body to head.

'It's like chopping down a tree,' they told me. 'You don't start at the top of the tree, you start at the bottom. You break the bottom, and the top will fall.'

I was ready. He was good alright, but I knew that I could do this. We touched gloves and the bell rang for round one. Instead of keeping his distance, he ran straight across the ring and tried to jump all over me, unloading a flurry of shots. *Happy days,* I thought, *let's go.* I banged him with straight right hands and left hooks, and his head was being jerked back, and then the referee stepped in and gave him a count.

I was like a lion stalking its prey now, smelling the blood of a wounded animal. According to my Dad, this was the thing that set me apart from my brothers. They were very good boxers, but when they had guys hurt, they tended to let their opponents off the hook. Not me. If I hurt you and smelled victory, I would be in to finish the job as quick as I could. I had that 'natural killer instinct', as my Dad used to call it.

The bell saved Robert at the end of round one, but he only had a minute to get himself in order before I was hunting him down again. In round two, the referee stepped in and pulled me off Robert to end the fight.

People were right – it was a challenge. But I showed them that when faced with a challenge, I was able to step up to the plate and deliver the same sort of performance as I did against the guys I was expected to beat.

It helped that at that time, CIE was one of the best clubs, if not *the* best club in the country at producing talent. We had champions at all age levels, and I had plenty of competition in the gym. I was challenged even to be the best kid in our club. We had the Clondalkin crew of the Jennings brothers, John Bailey, David Kelly and the Drumms. Then you had the Ballyfermot gang – Paul Stephens, the Marsh brothers and the Kennys. Plus there was the Maughan Family – there were five brothers – the McCanns – John and Alan, two big punchers – the Palmers, Kevin Darcy … The list goes on and on. I really could keep listing off names, guys that were as good as anyone else in the country.

The great thing about having all of this talent in the gym was the fantastic sparring that I was getting, day in, day out. The Maughans and Paul Stephens were superb for my development. They were at a similar level to myself, and Paul, well, he was my equal. He was a year older than me and, like myself, he was beating all around him. Like myself, he won all the national titles coming up through the ranks. And when we went to international level, I won two European bronze medals, but Paul had two European gold medals.

He was great for me. He was a tall southpaw, which meant that when I faced southpaws, who would normally cause orthodox, right-handed fighters problems, well, I had none. I was sparring with one of the best southpaws in Europe every day.

The ring in CIE was basically a matchbox, so you learned to fight very quickly. We were brought up with the ethos that what you do in training, you do in a fight, so we didn't mess around when we got inside that small ring to spar.

We were very competitive within our own group in the gym, but when a club from the outside came in, all bets were off. They were fair game. Peter taught his fighters to be ruthless, so when another club came down to CIE, we showed them no mercy. We were instructed to treat these fights just like we would treat a championship bout in the National Stadium. It's quite funny to think back on it. Peter would be standing on one side of the ring, and the coaches from the other club on the opposite side. We would touch gloves with whoever we were sparring against, and then proceed to beat them from one corner to the next. All the while, Peter would be shouting at you: 'Take it easy! Just move around.'

There would be bloody noses and tears, and guys just wanting to go home. My Grandad described us as animals, and often said that people would have paid good money just to come in and watch us training and sparring. And I suppose he was right – we were like animals. But that was the key to how we became so successful.

We also knew how to have fun while we trained. Often on runs, we would stop off at the local orchard and fill our pockets with apples. Climbing over the wall into the orchard and getting back out before the owner's dog got anywhere near chomping on us was easy enough; sneaking apples back into the gym was the tricky part. You needed this mix of seriousness and fun to be able to perform at the level we were trying to get to.

My first international tournament came about after I was selected to go into a box-off against Clive Smith of the Crumlin Boxing Club. One or other of us would go to the European Youths in Turkey. This competition is generally for sixteen-year-old boys, but the IABA would let me go, even though I was only fifteen, if I could beat the champion in the sixteen-year-old age group.

The Crumlin club really fancied their chances with this one. Smith was a good, strong, confident fighter, and also flashy at times. But we were very happy to take the chance and step up in age group to fight him. On the day, I gave one of the best boxing displays I had shown up to that point. As good as Clive was, and as confident as his team was, we won quite comfortably. From the opening bell, we controlled the fight and we won on all the judges' score cards. Turkey here we come.

I learned a valuable lesson out there. I boxed a Russian in the semi-final, and he was as strong as an ox. He looked like a man compared to me. He had facial hair, and I even think he had a bald spot. I thought, someone needs to check this guy's birth cert. The crowd were very pro-Russia as well, and hostile towards me. I had never experienced that before. Another thing I hadn't experienced before was a defeat. I learned from that fight that I still had a long way to go if I wanted to achieve the Olympic dream.

I travelled quite a bit from then on. Within two weeks of the tournament in Turkey, I was off to Canada to fight in the Gaelic Youths, and another fortnight later I was fighting in the Junior Olympics in Michigan, USA. As much as boxing is an individual sport, the friendships that we built up travelling away as a team, and the craic that we had, were just amazing. The camaraderie of the team was one of the things I grew to love about amateur boxing. We would be very focused on our boxing, and getting the right results, when we travelled to tournaments or single internationals, but once the fights were over, we got to sample what the country we were in had to offer in terms of fun. I got to travel the world by the time I was eighteen, and it was an amazing experience.

One of the best trips that I was on, in terms of boxing and having fun, was to New Zealand. We sent a team of eleven fighters out for two fights against the New Zealand national team. The events were to be held over two weeks, in Auckland and Christchurch. We marched out into the ring in Auckland as a team. I was already fully kitted out in my shorts, vest and gloves, ready to fight, as I was to be the first one in the ring after shaking hands with the New Zealand team and exchanging our national badges.

After everyone shook hands, or touched gloves in my case, both national anthems were played, and we made to exit the ring. We were told to hang on – the official ceremonial stuff wasn't over yet. Then the New Zealand team took positions in the ring in front of us and launched into the Haka, the traditional Maori war dance. It was absolutely amazing to see it first-hand and at such close quarters. The intensity of it, and the near-on foaming at the mouth that seemed to come with it, showed us that these men were ready for battle. I think I was covered in spit by the time they had finished it!

Everyone else then exited the ring, leaving just myself and my opponent and the referee. There was a big crowd; they had been buoyed up by the Haka and had become very vocal. I wasn't fazed by it – by this stage, I had learned to block noise out. We shaped up and touched gloves. Within about thirty seconds, my new New Zealand friend was starting to regret being so aggressive in his Haka welcome to me. In fairness to him, he lasted the three rounds, but he was going to be sore the next morning, that was for sure. I dominated him from start to finish.

We won the night 7-4 overall. That was a Friday night, and we were flying down to Christchurch the next day, and fighting the following Saturday down there against another New Zealand selection.

When we arrived in Christchurch, to our surprise, we found out that we were being sponsored by a pub/restaurant, and that they would be feeding us for the week while we were there. So there we were, a bunch of young lads, sitting around for a week waiting to fight, and spending a good amount of time, daily, in a pub. It was only going to go one way, and it didn't take long for it to happen.

We ended up getting to know the bar staff quite well. They were quite supportive of us having a fun time, and put security on all the doors so that whenever any of the management came around, we simply put our drinks away or moved to some other part of the bar, as it was a big place.

After being on the social all week, we were a little jaded going into our second encounter that Saturday. Funny enough though, I was boxing the same guy, and I ended up winning inside the distance this time. And overall, we beat them better the second time around, 8-3.

That was a good trip, but to be fair, trips like this were few and far between, and a long way away from my ambition of getting to the Olympic Games. For the next three years, this would be the sole focus of my attention.

Chapter 5

Chasing the Dream

I was just turning eighteen now, in February 1998, and we were starting to make plans for the 2000 Olympics in Sydney, Australia.

I had won my first Senior title, against Joe Burke from Wexford. He was trained by Billy Walsh, who we all know now as one of the most successful coaches in any sporting code in this country. Joe was a strong, game opponent, but he didn't get to see the final bell. I stopped him early in the fight, and I was the new Senior Champion at 54kg.

I went to my first major tournament as a senior soon afterwards, in Minsk, Belarus. I was beaten in my opening bout by Reidar Walstad from Norway. Our paths would eventually cross again. Of course, I was disappointed that I lost, but I was also very realistic about what my ultimate goal was. I was very much focused on the Olympic Games – these European Championships were just a building block towards that dream. It was experience that I was banking for a later date.

Not long after those championships, I sat down with my Dad and Peter to chat about what our plan was for the next few years. The conversation went back and forth on my weight division.

'He should stay at this weight – he is dominating here, and he knows these guys that he's fighting on the international scene,' said Peter, but Dad knew what the struggle was like for me at home.

'He won't be able to stay at this weight for the next two years, Peter,' he said. 'Sure, he's barely eating or drinking anything as it is. He can't keep this up.'

I generally stayed out of these conversations – I knew that they would come to the right decision for me.

Thankfully we, or they, came to the conclusion that it was best for me to move up to 57kg for the next National

Championships. I was relieved, to be honest. Making weight is never fun – you have to train hard to win tournaments, but doing it without putting any fuel in the system was not enjoyable! So, the plan now was to move up as soon as possible, and get as much experience and strength at 57kg as we possibly could before the Olympic Games.

This was the start of seriously chasing that Olympic dream, the dream I had had since I was eleven, winning my first All-Ireland title. Dad had his Olympic vest in a case in the attic, and I would often take it out.

'I want one of these, Dad,' I would say.

'You have one – that's yours, son,' he would say, but of course it wasn't the same.

The Irish Senior Championships of 1999 would be my first step towards that goal, my first big test at the new weight. The clear favourite for the title was Terry Carlyle. Terry had been there or thereabouts for the previous few years, and he was absolutely huge for the weight. For my skin-and-bone frame, Terry had a body builder's physique. He had muscle everywhere, or at least that's what it looked like to me.

The form book went according to plan, and Terry and were set to meet in the final.

'He's a big man, son,' my Dad would say over and over, 'You'll need to use all your boxing ability to keep him off you.'

'Yeah, I know, Dad. I heard you the first time,' I would reply. I was going to box, to use my brain and control the centre of the ring. I would need to be at the top of my game going in here if I wanted to win, and I would need to keep that little monster in my head, the one who loves to charge in and fight, under control.

The National Stadium was seriously noisy that night. That was partly because this was also a local rivalry – Terry was from Tallaght, and I was from Clondalkin. We were practically neighbours in west Dublin. We would also make a little bit of history that night, with the first female referee to run a Senior final fight. If you're going to start, you may as well start at the top.

Terry came out very much as expected. He stood big and tall, and tried to bully me around the ring. He would get as close as possible and then rough me up. I was jabbing, moving and throwing fast combinations to try to keep him off, but I wasn't always being successful. Terry was working his way inside, making things very awkward for me. Any time he got close enough, he would swing away, doing all he could to make life uncomfortable for me. He was pulling and leaning on me, or whacking me in close whatever way he could. That little monster inside me was starting to get awfully fed up with all of this.

I was two points up going into the last round. I knew that all I had to do was keep my distance and box to see home the victory. Terry, however, had other ideas. He came flying out of his corner and basically jumped right on top of me. He was crowding out my style, knocking me off my stride. I was getting more and more agitated, as I felt he was getting away with murder from the referee. He was holding on to me, hitting me on the back of the head, all of those rough-housing tactics.

The little voice inside my head was getting louder and louder, especially when Terry was holding me with one hand and began rubbing his other glove up against my face. That kind of hurts, especially the inside of the glove where the Velcro is. So I 'accidentally' gave Terry a bang of my head. Well, Sadie the referee saw that one alright. She stepped in to give me a public warning, which effectively meant she took two points off me. I was furious, and may have foolishly uttered a few words of displeasure in her direction, more in the heat of the moment than anything else. She could have given me another warning for that, but she didn't.

The fight was close now. The noise in the stadium had jumped up a few notches, to a deafening level. I forced myself to regain my focus, and landed a couple of combination shots in the few seconds that were left.

The bell went. The fight was over, and both of us raised our hands in triumph. But only one of us was going to be happy. I knew that the public warning could have a huge impact – not just on this fight, but on my whole life. The winner of this bout would get to go to the first set of qualifers for Sydney.

I felt I had done enough to win, and so did my corner. I walked back out to where the referee was waiting to shake both our hands, and to raise the hand of the winner. I had never been beaten in this country, and that's the way I wanted it to stay. The ring announcer called for a round of applause for both fighters, and the crowd obliged enthusiastically. He then announced the result:

'Ladies and gentlemen, after three rounds of boxing, we have a score of 7-7.'

Oh no, I thought, *this can't be happening!*

'We have a winner,' continued the announcer, 'after a countback.' This is where they take all the scores that the judges have individually entered, and then take the average of all those scores.

'On a score of 43-34, the 1999 National Senior Champion at 57kg is ...' It was only a matter of a second, but it felt like an eternity, '... in the red corner, Bernard Dunne.'

Phew! Relief flooded over me. Terry was devastated, of course, but better him than me. This was the first big step in chasing the dream. Olympic qualifiers here I come.

The World Championships was the first qualifier, to take place in Houston, Texas. The top eight fighters would get the golden ticket to the Olympics. My first bout was against a Dutch opponent, who I beat comfortably, but I came undone against my next opponent, a Czech who beat me on points.

Nicolas Cruz, our national coach, gave me the same talk that I would regularly get from Dad and Peter: 'Why are you fighting, Bernard? Just keep distance between you, and pick them off.'

Still though, no need to panic just yet. There would be another couple of chances to get there.

Next came a tournament in Tampere, Finland. I boxed a Russian in my first fight. A very tricky southpaw, but I had grown up with southpaws. I handled him well, and got the decision on points. I then came up against Falk Huste of Germany. He must have been at least six feet tall. I remember standing beside him and thinking, 'How the hell are you making weight?' I was only five-foot-seven, and the weight was a challenge for me, so it must have been an absolute nightmare for Falk.

The bout started off cagey enough, with the two of us sizing each other up. I was trying to stay as far away as possible, but then, when I did attack, I tried to get in as close as I could, to nullify his reach advantage. I figured that if I got in close enough, I could do some damage. The problem was that in getting in close, I came into his punching range, and Falk was intent on causing some damage of his own. He got me with a right hand that I never saw coming, and it put me on my backside. I was also cut by that shot, on my left cheek. I didn't know it then, but I would be thankful for this cut at a later stage in life.

The referee walked me over to the doctor so that he could check the cut, and the doctor stopped the fight. The cut was below the eye, which meant that there was no real danger of it causing me any problems during the fight. I couldn't believe that he stopped my fight. I was livid. The dream I was chasing seemed to be getting further away all the time now.

I won another National Senior title in the meantime, beating Happy Phillips from Athy in another early victory.

Not having a lot of competition at home was now starting to cause me some problems. It was all fine and dandy, winning national titles year in, year out, but I would need to be pushed and challenged at home if I was to succeed on the international scene.

My last chance to qualify was now coming up quickly. March 2000 was the date, and Venice in Italy was the destination. If I was going to do this, it looked like I was going to have to do it the hard way. I was hoping for the pretty, romantic ending, but I would take it any way I could at this stage. My first fight was against a Czech, Konstantin Flachbart. I caught him with a beautiful left hook to the body in the second round and he hit the floor. Game over. Nice start. I was in the zone. I was one-hundred-percent focused on this task. Nothing else in the world mattered at this moment in time.

My next opponent would be an Armenian, Artyom Simonyan. This guy was a little trickier than Flachbart. I was trailing on the judges' score card going into the third, but I eventually caught up with him.

I was into the semi-final now, and this was the bout that mattered most. If I won this, I would get that golden ticket.

I boxed Joni Turunen of Finland. This was it. My big moment. But once again, I went behind on the score card. *Stick to the plan and keep boxing,* I told myself. I knew I was boxing well, but the judges seemed to disagree. It was time, once again, to allow that little monster inside me to come out and go on the offensive. I dropped Turunen with a big right hand, but he got back to his feet. I went in for the kill, but the bell clanged after a few seconds, before I got a real chance to cause any more damage. I felt, though, that I had done enough to win.

'Fighters, centre of the ring,' in that Italian accent. I couldn't understand the next words that were said, but when I saw Joni jumping up into the air I knew he wasn't jumping because he had lost.

That was it. My Olympic dream was over. To say it hurt would be an understatement. The hardest part of it all was the phone call to Dad. He had wanted it for me as badly as I craved it for myself. He had put so much time into helping me chase down this dream that I felt I had let him down. As always, when I called, he was only worried about how I was, but I knew by his voice that he was disappointed.

It was no consolation to me that when Joni won the gold medal, it qualified me as 'first reserve' for the Games. That meant that I would get to compete if a boxer in my weight division got injured or dropped out. Really, it was more wishful thinking than anything else.

I arrived home on the afternoon of 2 April, and went out that evening for a few drinks with my brothers and a few friends. William, myself and Marsey, a friend from school who ended up marrying my sister, went on to a club.

It was here that my life would change forever, and boxing was responsible for it. While I went to get a drink, William got chatting to a friend of his girlfriend, and she asked who he was there with.

'My brother,' he said.

'Where is he?' she asked.

'That's him, coming over now.'

We were introduced, and we chatted for a while. And then we chatted for another while. Her friends ended up coming over to look for her.

We exchanged phone numbers, and myself and Pamela are now fourteen years married. Later, she told me that she had been to a fortune teller that week. She was told that she would be introduced to a man very soon with a scar on his cheek, and that he would be her soulmate. That could have been half of Dublin in fairness, but still I was thankful to Falk Huste for inflicting that scar on me, no more than a few months beforehand.

I believe that everything, good and bad, happens for a reason. I would never have been out that night if I had qualified for the Olympic Games. Things happen to all of us throughout our lives, good luck and bad luck, but it is how you deal with these situations that really matters. It has been said that 'for every door that closes, another two open'. I firmly believed that then, and I most certainly still believe it today.

I travelled out to the Sydney Olympics with Michael Roche, who was our only boxing qualifier, and Nicolas Cruz and Martin Power.

My Olympic dream became a nightmare when I travelled out there. Firstly, I cracked some metacarpals, tiny bones in my right hand, and then I got a gash above my left eye that required fifteen stitches. And it really just went downhill from there. Because I was injured, I was no longer allowed to stay in the Olympic village. There was nowhere else for me to stay, and I was unable to change my tickets and just go home. A family from Cork – the O'Driscolls, friends of Michael Roche – put me up. I don't know what I would have done if they hadn't.

It all soured the taste in my mouth for amateur boxing, and for the Olympics. I made up my mind that I would never box as an amateur again. My next decision was whether to turn professional or to throw in the towel and go back to college.

But all of that was still ahead of me. For now, I was travelling home from Sydney, dejected but hopeful for the future. I had spoken to my Dad, and we would start to plan after a short break.

I may not have got the dream that I was chasing, but because of that failure, I ended up finding my wife. But still, man, I wish I had got the Olympics!

Chapter 6

False Dawn

So, I spent a couple of months sitting and thinking, figuring out what I wanted to do next and where I saw my future. Dad liked the fact that I had gone back to college, exploring new opportunities and avenues for my future. But boxing was still calling. Harry Hawkins, who I had trained with several times in his club, was in my ear about turning professional. 'It is made for you, Bernard,' he'd say. 'There are people out there who will be willing to pay to get involved with you.'

My Dad, as always, was a big part of this, and Harry, who I had built up a good relationship with, was an excellent second voice. The decision to turn pro was finally made.

As much as I loved representing my country and travelling with the Irish national boxing team, it was time to move on. I was never going to achieve the Olympic dream, but maybe, just maybe, I could become Champion of the World.

Harry was already involved in the professional side of the game. A couple of fighters from his Holy Trinity gym in Belfast had already turned pro. They had signed with managers Panos Elidos and Frank Maloney. At the time, amongst others, Panos and Frank managed Lennox Lewis, who was Heavyweight Champion of the World.

It was a very straightforward negotiation process for me. Panos and Frank were involved with several world champions; they had a television deal; but what really sealed the deal for me was that they had Harry Hawkins. Harry was someone I already enjoyed working with, but it was only over the next decade that I would see what a good man he was.

Brian Magee, one of Harry's other fighters, was fighting in Peterborough in England against Neil Linford, competing for the IBO inter-continental super-middleweight title. Here I was in the Bushfield leisure centre, seated between Frank and Panos. The fight was being shown on television on Sky Sports, and I was basically being paraded around in front of the media as the new kid on the block. This was it. This was the new dream. I was about to hit the big time. I was being treated like a king, and I liked how it felt.

At the end of the night, after Brian won a hard-fought points victory, Panos turned to me and said, 'That will be you soon. We are all very excited about this deal, Bernard.' They were excited, and I was over the bloody moon.

We all went for dinner after the fight. Everyone at the table was laughing and joking, looking forward to the future and what lay in store for us. All that was left now was for me to have my routine medical tests, which would consist of a general health check and an MRI brain scan. I couldn't wait to tell the lads when I got home. 'Great, we'll get a couple of nice little holidays out of this,' they said. 'Vegas, here we come!'

Professor Jack Phillips conducted the medical tests in Beaumont hospital in Dublin. Jack is a very nice, chatty man, which was good as I quite like to natter away a bit myself. I would never had anticipated though, after this first meeting, the important role that Jack would end up playing in my life.

I had to go back to get my results from Jack a couple of days after taking the scan. I bounced my way into his office, ready to pick up my medical report and get started on my path to becoming Champion of the World, but I left the office feeling quite confused and bewildered. Jack informed me that I had a cyst on my brain. It lay neatly between the two halves of the brain. Jack said that this was perfectly normal, that more than likely it was something I was born with. As I walked out of his office, he said that it was nothing to worry about.

I went home and rang Harry, relaying to him what I could remember from my conversation with Jack. The silence at the other end of the phone was deafening.

Then he said, 'Are you serious? Don't mess about with something like this, Bernard.' I knew by the way he said my first name, much like a parent when they are giving out to you, that he wasn't terribly pleased with the news.

'I am serious, Harry,' I told him. 'Jack assured me that it was really nothing out of the ordinary.' Well, at least that was what I thought he was saying. At this stage, I could sense that Harry was starting to get frustrated that my answers to him weren't clearer.

'Look, I'll call him myself,' he said.

It was only now that I started to feel that this may be a little more sinister than I had thought. I told my parents what Jack had said, and what Harry was saying, and I could see shock and worry on their faces. Mom began to cry, and started blaming herself for this little space in my brain. You see, when I was much younger, I mean when I was a toddler, my Mam was changing my nappy on the table one day, and, for one second, she turned her back on my little mischievous infant self.

Even as a baby, I thought I was invincible, and I flung myself off the table. Unfortunately, I hadn't developed my superpowers at this stage of my life, and I cracked my head on the solid floor. I ended up on my first of many visits to Our Lady's Hospital, with a fractured skull.

'Actually, Ma, you know what? Yeah, it probably is from that,' wasn't the right thing to say at this delicate moment! She became hysterical. Dad told me to stop, and eventually calmed her down. The next couple of hours were a little uncomfortable in the Dunne household, as I sat waiting for Harry to call back.

The phone rang and the whole house seemed to hold its breath as I went to answer it.

'Hello?'

'Bernard, it's Harry,' he said, as if I wouldn't recognise his thick Northern accent. 'Listen, we are going to have to be very careful with this. If this breaks,' he continued, 'you may never box again.'

'What? Seriously?'

'Look, I'm coming down to Dublin. We'll chat more then.'

He arrived at the house later that evening. It was one of the longest days of my life. The words 'you may never box again' just kept running through my head.

'Jack thinks this is something you were born with,' said Harry.

'Well, that's okay then, isn't it?' I said.

'It's not, Bernard,' he replied, again with the first name! 'The British Boxing Board of Control has a zero-tolerance policy when it comes to anything like this, Bernard. They've had a couple of scares – Gerald McClellan and Michael Watson both suffered brain injuries in the last number of years in British boxing rings, and they are worried about another incident like this.'

What, me? A brain injury? What? I'm sure Harry could see all this going through my mind.

'The only people who know about this right now are me, you, your Mam and Dad and the professor. The only person he has told is Mel Christle.' Mel was, and still is, the President of the Boxing Union of Ireland, which runs professional boxing in this country.

Both Mel and Professor Jack had said they would not release the results of the scan, as they knew what could happen if they did. Both men were as good as their word.

Harry stayed in Dublin that night, and we met up again the next day. Jack wanted to meet us all. We chatted about the results and what they meant. As far as Jack was concerned, the cyst was most probably something I was born with. But the fact was, I had never had a brain scan before, so he could not prove it for certain. If I had had a scan before, I could have compared it to this one, and if there was no change in it, it would prove that it was something I was born with.

The plan now was that I would go to the United States, and start my professional career over there. The Americans were a little less strict with their medical rules.

There was only one problem with this plan: We had already gone through long talks with Panos and Frank, and had all but signed a contract with them. They had courted me for a long time, and had offered me a great deal. They were now just waiting for a phone call to say when I would be coming over to sign the contract. Who was going to tell them the bad news? Thankfully Harry drew the short straw on this one.

Harry went and told Panos that I had got a better offer from the States, and I wasn't going to change my mind. To say that Panos was annoyed at hearing this news would be an understatement. He completely lost the plot. He wanted to make a counter-offer, but Harry told him it was a done deal and there was no turning back. Myself and Panos have never crossed paths again.

Our next challenge would be to find a promoter in the States who would offer me a similar deal. This proved a little harder than we had thought it would, and it also took a lot longer than we expected.

One man had been in the background while all of this was going on – Brian Peters. He was a young and ambitious man, with a love for boxing. I had known Brian since I was fifteen years old. Back then, he had watched me win my Youth 1 national title. When I got out of the ring, Brian sent one of his men, Tommy McQuillan, to my changing room to ask if I would meet him. Dad said, 'Yeah, no problem.'

I was still in my fight gear when Brian came in and congratulated me on my win. Then he asked me if I would have any interest in going over to Luttrellstown Castle and sparring with Wayne McCullough. I had barely broken a sweat in my fight, so I said, 'Spar with Wayne McCullough? Yeah, I'd love to.' This was my usual 'I'll get in the ring with anyone' attitude. The fact that the other person in the ring would be the World Champion himself was a great honour for me, even though I probably didn't show it at the time.

We travelled to the hotel where he was training, and there he was, warming up and shadow boxing: Wayne McCullough, the Pocket Rocket, Olympic silver medallist and current World Champion. He was everything that I wanted to become, and an absolute gentleman, as I would find out. We sparred a couple of rounds. I survived, thankfully, to be able to go into school the following Monday and tell all my mates who I had been in the ring with. Myself and Wayne have been good friends since then, and he was really valuable to me at a later stage in my life.

So, from this point on, Brian Peters had been in my ear about turning professional. He kept in touch over the next few years, and wanted to be involved in my career. I wasn't overly keen on it back then, but maybe now was the right time to see if the two of us could work together. I went to

Brian and told him the whole story. If we were going to work together, I wanted to be upfront from the start, so that he knew what he was dealing with. The news of the cyst didn't scare him off, and he set about working to find me a deal in the United States of America.

As I said earlier on: 'For every door that closes, another two open.' To be honest, I was just glad to be getting a chance to see if I had what it took to compete as a pro.

Chapter 7

Los Angeles, Baby

It was November 2001, and we were all silent on the drive to the airport. I may have been starting out on my new career, a great new adventure, but I was leaving an awful lot behind, and that's what I was feeling in the car. The family and some friends were all coming along to say goodbye. The mood was a powerful mixture of laughter, excitement and sadness. Redser was excited for me. 'I'll be over soon enough,' he promised.

Pamela and my Dad were fairly moody. I could sense that their smiles weren't as warm as the others when we were leaving the house. I could understood my Dad not being too happy. He was letting go of his son, but he was also losing his fighter. My Dad had trained and shaped me since I could walk. We had spent so much time together, so many great times and hard times, and now I was leaving for pastures new. He wasn't just my Dad; we had become great friends and we were able to speak to each other in ways that only we could understand. He was emotional, and I could feel it.

I tried making jokes to lighten the mood. I think I started singing, 'I'm leaving on a jet plane, don't know when I'll be back again.' Okay, I know I'm not the greatest singer in the world, but it wasn't so bad that they had to start crying.

Actually, Pamela had been crying since we set out for the airport. This was a little more confusing to me, as she was going to follow me out to America in six weeks' time. A simple kiss, 'I'll call you when I land', and 'I love you' was what I left her with. That all got a worse reaction than the singing!

But this was it – the first step towards the dream of being a World Champion. I had told Barry McGuigan, when I was six years old, that someday I would be Champion of the World.

In chasing any dream, tough choices have to be made, and this was one of those choices. I had to leave the comforts of home, my family and my friends. But this wasn't a sacrifice I was making. It was a choice. I knew it was the right thing to do, but it was still extremely hard. I said all my goodbyes, and headed for the emigration gate. Just like inside the boxing ring, I was going to have to face this one by myself.

There is nothing like an eleven-hour flight, all on your own, to make the full weight of what you have just done sink in. It was really only now that I was starting to realise what I was doing. I was moving thousands of miles away from all that I knew. I hadn't thought about it too much at home. I was so focused on getting my deal, and on starting a pro career, that I just sort of glossed over the bits in the middle. Now I had eleven long hours, with no one else to talk to, just to sit and think.

It didn't scare me though. I was excited by it. I had spoken with Steve Collins and Wayne McCullough, and they both told me I was being given the chance to train in one of the best gyms in the world, with one of the best coaches in the world. When boxing legends like those men tell you that you're doing the right thing, you tend to sit up and take notice.

Coming down to land into Los Angeles, the first thing you notice is how big everything is. I was trying to take it all in — after all, this would be my home for the next few years. Walking through the arrival gate at the airport, I was looking around for a sign with my name on it. I was told that I would be picked up at the airport. I looked around at the many cards with names on them for collection, but there wasn't one that said 'Bernard Dunne'. Then out of somewhere, I hear 'Bearnaarrd … Bearnaarrd Dunne'. I understood the 'Dunne' part, but was a bit confused by the 'Bearnaarrd' part.

I found where the voice was coming from — a giant of a man, who asked me, 'Are you the boxer Bearnaarrd Dunne?' I figured it was me he was talking about. The 'Bearnaarrd' pronunciation was throwing me, but I figured it was something I would get used to. 'That's me,' I said with a smile, and I reached out my hand. The man was Macka Foley, an Irish-American. I know loads of Americans call themselves Irish-Americans, but with a name like Foley, there had to be a real connection.

'I reckoned it was you,' he said. 'You have the walk and the look of a fighter.' He told me he was from the Wildcard gym, and was here to pick me up. Freddie Roach, who would be my trainer, was away with one of his other fighters, but he would be back in a couple of days. Macka took both my cases and tossed them into the back of his old Chevy. The car was as big as a tank, but it had seen better days. We hopped in and, as we drove off, Macka told me how delighted he was that they finally had 'another Irish guy in the gym'. He wanted to collect me today, as he was part-Irish, and he felt it was his 'duty' to be the one to welcome me to America.

I knew straight away that he was a good guy. He chatted all the way to the gym, but after about two minutes I completely zoned out and was in a world of my own, watching LA glide by through the car window. As we pulled up to the gym, Macka told me that this was where I would be staying for the next while.

'At the gym?' I said, in some shock.

'No,' Macka laughed. 'Not the gym, the motel next door.'

The motel was called the Vagabond Inn, and it most certainly wasn't a place I would want to stay too long. It looked like a relic from the 1970s, with a huge, pink neon sign and old, tattered insides. It looked like it hadn't had a lick of paint for a couple of decades. My mates had said I would be living the high life in LA. They all envied me ... If they could only see me now.

I checked in to my 'hotel', dropped my cases in the room and went straight to work. As I walked up the corrugated-steel stairs to the Wildcard, I could hear the sounds of people punching bags and skipping ropes, and trainers barking out instructions. I felt right at home. As I walked in through the big black cast-iron door, I spotted Macka in the ring, doing mitts with one of his weekly keep-fitters.

A little grey-haired man with a limp and tattoos on nearly all of his visible skin came toward me. 'Hey, Irish, welcome to the jungle,' he said. This was Peppa Roach, Freddie Roach's brother. He had been a fighter himself in his younger days, and had had a couple of professional fights. I think he may have had more outside the ring than inside. He did some time in prison, and got mixed up with gangs in there just to survive. That's where all the tattoos came from.

When he got out of prison, Freddie looked after Peppa, getting him to come to his gym and train people. It was a good little earner for him – ten dollars to do some mitts or pads with someone for ten minutes. If you trained one of the many famous guys who came into the gym, well then, that was big bucks. They would pay to make sure you stayed with them for the whole session. The gym was full of coaches like Peppa and Macka. Good guys, if a little crazy, working hard to make a living from the beautiful game that is boxing.

A loud bell sounded to end the round. Macka turned around and spotted me. 'What you doing here, man?' he said. He thought I should be resting after my eleven-hour flight. I thought differently. I wanted to get straight to it.

After all I had been through to get here, I didn't want to waste any time. Plus, my new home next door didn't feel all that homely, and anyway, what else was I going to do? I knew nobody here, and we were out in the middle of Hollywood. Hollywood has been done up in recent years, but back then, it wasn't the safest place to be. There were huge problems with gangs and guns and drugs, and all that comes with that. It was not a great place for sightseeing.

I was excited to see what this gym had to offer. What made it so special? I was half-expecting to see some fancy machines and gadgets. Maybe a big changing room, with lockers and deluxe showers. Remember, I had gone through the last fifteen years training in a cold gym with holes in the walls and ceiling, and freezing showers that would make you wash yourself in world-record time.

So, as you can imagine, I was slightly disappointed when I saw that this was just like any gym I had seen in Dublin. Nothing special, no fancy gadgets, no comfortable changing room and no deluxe showers! I was quickly reminded of what my Dad always said when we complained about the leaks coming in through the roof in CIE: 'It's not the gym that makes the fighter; it's the discipline, dedication and a willingness to learn.' He was never far wrong, my old man.

I trained all that weekend. In between training sessions, I would pop across to one of the many fast-food restaurants on the block. Not ideal food for a professional athlete, but without my own apartment, and with no kitchen to cook in, it was just about making the best of the situation.

The worst part of my first couple of days was the boredom in between sessions. These were the days before everyone had a smartphone, and I had to go out to a payphone down the road to call home. There wasn't much sleeping done either, as there was constant noise from the street outside the hotel, from traffic, cops' sirens and people just roaring at each other. It wasn't the ideal start that I had hoped for.

Freddie Roach arrived into the gym on Monday. As I was staying right beside the gym, I was the first through the doors that morning. I was met with a big smile. Freddie always seemed to be happy.

'Bernard!' he said. 'Good to meet you finally, sorry I wasn't here when you arrived, but I had to look after one of my guys.'

I told him not to worry, and that I was glad he could pronounce my name properly. He asked how I was getting on, and what did I think of LA? 'Crazy' was the first word that sprang to mind to describe it, or at least the little bit that I had gotten to see. He just laughed.

Freddie had been given a couple of my fights to watch on DVD, and Steve Collins had spoken to him about me. He had obviously liked what he saw, as here I was in LA, about to start my professional career with him. But I still wanted to make a big impression now that I was here.

Freddie wrapped my hands before we got going. He put as much attention into the hand wrapping as a mother would, making sure that her child was wrapped good and tight in their coat and scarf and gloves before going outside. It was like an artist at work, looking after his masterpiece, making sure that not one stroke was misplaced. I commented on how much care he was putting into wrapping my hands, and Freddie said, 'These are the tools of your trade, Bernard. Remember that. Without your tools, you get no work done, and if you get no work done, you make no money.' It was slowly starting to sink in that this was a business and, like any business, you have to look after your assets. That's exactly what Freddie was doing – he was looking after his assets.

So here I was, about to do my first session with legendary trainer Freddie Roach. I skipped for ten minutes to warm up, and then got into the ring to do some shadow boxing. I was the only boxer there at the time, so I had Freddie's complete focus. He stood at the side of the ring, leaning on the top rope.

He watched as I danced around the ring, throwing my jab, then double-jab followed by combinations. I was relentless, my feet and hands in constant motion. The bell rang and I walked to the corner, where Freddie had a water bottle waiting for me. I was feeling good, having just bounced around the ring and thrown my best shots as fast as I could. Happy out. He must have been impressed.

'What's the rush?' he said, stepping through the ropes. 'Settle; take your time; pick your shots.'

For the next four rounds of shadow boxing, and then six rounds of mitts, it was like getting a lesson in the classroom. Except that this was a boxing ring, and my teacher was one of the best in the world. What struck me was how he spoke with you about what *you* were doing, and how he felt you might be able to improve your way of doing it. It was all about your way of doing it. He didn't try to shape you into what he thought a boxer should look like. He tried to help you improve the style that you already had, and work with that.

I may not have felt at home in my environment outside of the gym, but there in the ring with Freddie, it felt like I was in the kitchen with my Dad. Like this was where I should be. We finished up our session with some core work and a little skipping just to cool down. I showered up and hung around the gym for a bit for a chat with Freddie.

The conversation turned to why I was staying in the hotel, or 'motel' as they called it. 'Why wasn't there a place lined up for you when you got here?' Freddie asked. I didn't have an answer to that, but Freddie said, 'Never mind. But one thing is for sure, you need to get yourself out of there as soon as possible.'

I didn't have a clue where to start looking, so Freddie suggested one or two areas. He mentioned that one of them was beside the beach.

'Which place is that?' I said.

'Santa Monica,' was his reply.

So I picked up the *Los Angeles Daily News*, checked the listings for properties to rent and jumped on the Big Blue Bus to Santa Monica.

Chapter 8

No More False Starts

Stepping off the bus in Santa Monica, it seemed like I had travelled to a completely different world from the one I had just left behind in Hollywood. Palm trees lined the streets, people of all ages were cruising around on skateboards, and the smell of the ocean all around was amazing. This was the California I had imagined when I left Neilstown.

Armed with the local paper, I set off in search of a new home. Having gotten myself slightly lost, I stopped a man to ask for directions. 'Whereabouts back home are you from?' he asked me in a thick Dublin accent. It turns out that the first guy I asked for directions was actually from Dublin. We had some small chat about home, and what I was doing in America. Then he told me that he was heading home for a bit, and that if I wanted to, I could sublet his place. The address was '7th and California'. We went to see it, and that was that. I had my first home in Santa Monica.

The next big event on my horizon was just over five weeks away, 19 December to be exact. This was the day when the world would see professional boxer Bernard Dunne in action. From now until that date, I needed to get the head down and work hard without any distractions. I had to make sure I was in the best possible shape, as you only get one chance to make a first impression.

Getting into good shape was not going to be a problem when I had the likes of Willie Jorrin, Israel Vasquez and the now-legendary Manny Pacquiao to train with every day. It was the best environment possible in which to grow and learn as a fighter. The Wildcard gym was constantly buzzing, full of life and excitement, with some of the best boxers on the planet training there.

I travelled every day on the bus up Santa Monica Boulevard. It would take about an hour, and I would jump off on the corner of Hollywood Boulevard and Vine Street, directly facing the gym. Getting the bus wasn't for the faint-hearted, if the truth be told. There would often be people fighting with each other, fighting with the driver or sometimes just fighting with themselves. It was that type of town. The bus was my only form of transport at the time, so I just got on with it.

We travelled up to Oroville in northern California on Monday, 17 December, as my fight was a midweek fight, on the Wednesday. It was being shown live on Fox Sports television channel, which was a big boost for me. This was a great opportunity, to perform not just for the people who were there to watch it in person, but also to impress the audience watching in the comfort of their own homes.

Rodrigo Ortiz was the fighter I would face in the ring. He was a journeyman boxer, who was brought in to give a kid like me some experience as I stepped up through the levels in the professional game. I finished him inside two rounds. It was the perfect start, and more importantly, it was sending me home happy for Christmas.

I hopped on a plane on 21 December. I had only been gone for two months, but it felt like a lot longer. Thankfully it wasn't just me who felt that way; I think Pamela missed me a little too. It was the last time that we would be apart, as Pamela was going to travel back over with me in January.

Being home was great. Paddy and myself got away with a couple of nights of being social together. It was like we hadn't seen each other in years! It was a short stay at home though, as I wanted to get back to business as soon as possible.

When we got back to LA, we got some bad news. My promoter, America Presents, had gone out of business. I trained every day, but it was hard with no promoter and so no fights coming up. No fights meant no money, and no money meant stress and worry about what I was going to do next.

We were lucky that we made friends with an Irish family who had left Belfast and set up home in Orange County. They were really a great support network, both for myself and Pamela.

One day, out of the blue, I had gotten a call from an unknown American. 'Hi, is this Ben?' said the voice at the other end of the phone.

'Yes, who is this?' I asked.

'I am Jimmy Antolin,' came the reply. 'My wife's family are all from Belfast. A friend of yours, Harry Hawkins, gave them a call and asked them would they just keep an eye on you.' They were as good as their word and so Jimmy called. He arranged to come over and pick us up the next day.

Jimmy arrived outside our apartment the next morning in a big pickup truck. He was not what I was expecting. A big, well-built, Mexican-looking man, he had somehow managed to get himself mixed up with a family from Belfast. 'Hey, Ben, great to meet you, brother,' were the words that greeted us as we opened our door. 'All the family is coming over to ours for a barbeque, so let's get on the road.'

We set off with Jimmy, not really sure what to expect. One thing myself and Pamela did not expect was that it would take over an hour-and-a-half to get to his house. Jimmy drove all that way just to bring us to meet his family.

The whole family was there, and they all came out to meet us. It was funny to hear the Belfast-American twang when Pat and Marie spoke. They were the originals of the family, who had made the move over to the States.

They gave us big hugs, and welcomed us into their family. Marie told me that her brother Eddie Shaw had helped train Barry McGuigan. They understood boxing, and they had some Irish blood in them. These were definitely my type of people. Jimmy would make the three-hour round trip every weekend after that for the next couple of months to bring us up to his family and make us feel welcome. To this day, we are still friends. They really helped myself and Pamela through a difficult time.

One bright note eventually came from home – a group of businessmen were going to help out by sponsoring me, to keep me going in the States.

It took me eight months to get legal problems sorted out with my old promoter. Eight months! I should have had four or five fights in that length of time. But now, finally, I was free and I could start looking for a new deal.

One day, a message came in that SRL Boxing were looking for an opponent for an up-and-coming prospect they were working with, a guy from the Dominican Republic. 'Freddie, have you got a guy, around 126 to 130lbs, for one of our guys?' was the question. Now, this was a guy that SRL Boxing were investing in; they didn't expect him to be beaten. Freddie thought hard about it. In the end, he decided, 'The kid needs a fight. He's been training for eight months now, he needs to be let loose.' We agreed to the fight.

It turned out that 'SRL' stood for Sugar Ray Leonard. In case you don't recognise the name, this man was a living legend. He had won a gold medal at the 1976 Montreal Olympic Games, the same Olympics that my Dad had competed in. He was a World Champion at five different weight divisions.

I grew up watching this man and trying to copy his style and his moves. Now here I was, getting a chance to fight in front of him against one of his guys. *This guy must be good,* I thought, *if Sugar Ray is looking at him.*

But I was no slouch. I was more than ready for this, and hungry for an opportunity to fight again. ESPN television were showing the fight live on TV, so this was really a big opportunity.

When I got into the ring that night, I saw a man-mountain standing across from me in the other corner. *I must have come out for the wrong fight,* I thought. *This guy is huge.* But no, I was in the right place, and this was my opponent, Christian Cabrera. He was just a big slab of muscle, and here I was, all skin and bone.

We were called in to the centre of the ring by the referee to touch gloves, and then back to our corners. Justin Fortune, who travelled with me as Freddie was away, gave me a high five. 'Work off that jab, and whip that hook into the body,' he told me.

Easy for you to say, I thought, *when you're getting out of the ring. I'm the one that has to stand and fight the Incredible Hulk!*

Ding ding! The bell went and I walked out to the centre of the ring. Cabrera came springing out from his corner.

I threw out my left jab and *boom!* I came across with a big right over the top, and nailed Cabrera on the chin. He hit the floor. He got up on the count of four, but his legs were starting to do a merry dance of their own. He was all over the place.

The referee somehow allowed the fight to continue. My little bit of inexperience showed, as I tried to jump all over Cabrera to end the fight, when I should have taken my time and been a little more calculated about it. I wouldn't make that mistake a second time.

Cabrera came out for the second round, trying to make a fight of it. I was jabbing and moving, waiting for the right moment to land that big shot. My back was on the ropes as Cabrera tried to trap me and land a few shots, but I leaned back on the rope and then sprang forward with another thunderous right hand. This sent Cabrera crashing to the floor, and brought the crowd to their feet.

Sugar Ray was very quickly into the ring. He may have been disappointed that Cabrera wasn't the fighter he thought he was, but Ray had already moved on. Now he was looking at this 'scrawny Irish kid', as one of the commentators called me, who could generate such knockout punching power. Ray came over to me in the ring.

'Wow, we have to talk,' he said.

You bet we do, Ray, I thought.

This was the break that I needed to kick-start my career.

We went for dinner that night – Ray and his team and me and my team. Everyone was in good spirits, and we left the dinner with the promise that SRL Boxing would have a contract for me within a couple of weeks. He was as good as his word, and we signed the contract in my apartment in Santa Monica a couple of weeks later. A fight was then organised for me, on the undercard of the great American heavyweight, 'Baby' Joe Mesi.

Excitement was rushing through my veins at the thought of fighting in front of 17,000 people in the sold-out arena. I would have to do a full medical for this fight, including another MRI scan. Having completed all of this in LA, I travelled to Buffalo, New York, ready to launch my career again.

At the weigh-in before the fight, I noticed that a row had broken out between Ron Katz, who worked for SRL, and an officer of the New York State Athletic Commission, Barry Jordan. They weren't looking at me, but I had a sneaking feeling that I could be getting some bad news soon.

'You can't seriously be doing this to me,' Ron said at the top of his voice. I walked over to where the row was happening.

The Commissioner was saying, 'I want to see this kid when he is old and grey, and has children and grandchildren of his own.'

Ron Katz turned to me. 'Ben, the scan has shown up some white matter on your brain. Until they can do further scans, you're not going to be able to box.' I was put on a complete ban, not just from fighting, but from entering any gym, until further tests were carried out.

I stayed calm throughout all of this, as I had heard it all before, but now the public were going to hear about it. A couple of articles appeared in newspapers at home that spoke about risks of 'paralysis', or even 'death', if I continued to box. Mammy wasn't too happy at reading all of this, of course, but I was relaxed about it. I spoke with Professor Jack, and he was sure that I would come through the tests okay, and that I would box again. But this was yet another false start that I did not need. I was growing more and more impatient as time went on.

Thankfully, Freddie wasn't overly concerned, and he continued to train me. But I found it really hard to stay focused. After a couple of weeks, Pamela and myself decided that we would go home and wait for the results of the tests I had taken. So off we went, with some parting words from Freddie: 'Get back here as soon as you get the all-clear – we have some work to do.'

It was now the week before Christmas. Pamela and I were out at the cinema in Liffey Valley when my phone started to light up. It was Brian Peters.

'Hello,' I whispered in the dark cinema. 'Brian, are you there?'

There was no answer.

After a painfully long silence, Brian's voice came on the line:

'You need to get yourself back to the States as fast as you can. You've been cleared to fight.'

I had been acting all confident, but this was a massive relief to me. A part of me had feared that my dream of fighting in the professional ranks, on the big stage, had been taken away from me forever.

We had a good Christmas that year, and then it was time for Brian and SRL to give me the present that I wanted – fights, and plenty of them. Over the next six months, I would have six fights, with five KOs. TV companies were loving me. It helped that I had people like Sugar Ray Leonard and Freddie Roach backing me. I had eight fights in total that year, and then four the following year. I was now fighting ten-round fights, and headlined 'Boxing After Dark', a show on the major TV network Showtime.

I had come a long way, from that skinny kid in the CIE boxing club to being broadcast live on TV stations all over America. But now Pamela and I were thinking about going home. I felt that there was an opportunity in professional boxing back in Ireland. It had been a long time since professional boxing of a decent standard had been in this country, but I thought that maybe we could bring it back. Pamela and I were now married, and talking about having a family, and we wanted to do that in Dublin rather than in LA.

It was a risk that I was taking – leaving the States, where I had built up a reputation, to come back home. But it was a risk that I felt was worth taking. I was now out of contract with SRL, so it was a perfect time to see if it would work.

Brian set about finding a venue, and looking at whether there would be any interest from TV stations back home to support it. RTÉ came on board, and the National Stadium was chosen as the venue. My homecoming fight would be against UK boxer Jim Betts, on 19 February 2005. The boy was most certainly back in town.

This would be the start of something that I could never, in my wildest dreams, have predicted.

Chapter 9

Everyone Wants to Hug the Winner

I was being carried around the ring in the Point Depot (now the 3Arena) in front of a wildly cheering crowd. They were singing and dancing. We had had a massive win, and Dublin was celebrating the crowning of one of their own as the new Champion of Europe.

This was a huge scalp for me to take, a victory that pushed me up into the world's top ten ranked fighters at super-bantamweight. It was a little over twenty months since I had returned home, and I had now won twenty-two out of twenty-two fights as a professional boxer. RTÉ, the national broadcaster, were showing all my bouts live on television.

It had been a seriously busy time since I had left the States. 'What are you doing, coming back here?' people had asked me. 'Why would you leave Freddie Roach and SRL? Are you crazy?'

In the lead-in to my first fight on home soil, against Jim Betts, we were just hoping that people would take notice and give us some support. It was a big risk leaving America, and we hoped we had made the right move. Shortly after we announced the fight, ticket sales went through the roof, and they quickly sold out. Brian had managed to persuade RTÉ to show the fight on television, which would ensure that the Irish public got to see what we were doing.

The build-up to the Jim Betts fight was a new experience for me. There was a lot of media attention, and the Irish public seemed to be excited to find out what this lad from Neilstown had learned on his travels in America. I had to get used to all of this attention very quickly.

The changing rooms in the National Stadium, the official home of Irish boxing, had not changed since I first boxed there as an eleven-year-old, trying to win my first All-Ireland title. What *was* different though was that the stadium was packed to the rafters. There was standing room only, and even then it was a squeeze.

On the night, when Jim Betts made his way out to the ring, I could hear the booing from the crowd from my changing room. *I wouldn't like to be walking out into the middle of that,* I thought to myself.

Coming to fight in someone else's back yard takes guts. It can be pretty hostile, and this can throw an inexperienced fighter off their game. It can also give the home fighter that extra ten percent. My reception was very different, but I would not need that extra help on this occasion. I put him away in the fifth round, with a crisp left hook to the body.

Yuriy Voronin was next up. He was from Ukraine and had a bit of punch in him, which I was going to find out about shortly. It was a ten-round fight, and for nine-and-a-half of those rounds, I dominated. Then, with a minute left in the final round, he caught me with a straight left hand, clean in the chin. Silence fell upon the stadium. You could hear a pin drop. I think I would still be falling now if it wasn't for the ropes that caught me. He might have stopped my journey in its tracks there and then, if he hadn't been in such a rush to finish me off. Thankfully he was, and thankfully he was also tired.

He pushed me to the ground, which didn't take much now, and the referee, Emile Tiedt, son of 1956 Olympic silver medallist Fred Tiedt, was generous enough to give me plenty of time to get back to my feet. I would hit the deck another two times in those final seconds, none of which were counted as knockdowns. The crowd got as much of a fright as I did. I was let out of jail that night.

During the post-fight interview, my mind was still a blur. Harry stepped in and said, 'Okay, that's it, we have to go. Thanks, folks,' and cut short the interview. The next day, when I was back to my senses, I got a hell of a telling off from my Dad and Harry, about dropping my hands and playing to the crowd.

'What were you thinking? You were warned about playing to the crowd and trying to please everyone,' they said.

I didn't think I was that bad. It had just felt more natural for me to box that way. I realised though that if the quality of my opponents was going to keep improving, then my defence would also need to improve.

In the eight months after this fight, I would have plenty of time to demonstrate that I had been working on these skills. I had five fights in that time, which was busy by anybody's standards. This included two fights on foreign soil – one in Germany and the other in Italy. I was now being lined up for my first major challenge, a European title fight.

In the other corner would be Esham Pickering. Esham, a thirty-year-old from Sheffield in England, was trained by Brendan Ingle, a fellow Dubliner who had also trained Prince Naseem Hamed. Esham had fought at world-title level, and had been British, Commonwealth and European champion. He was coming to fight with a wealth of experience and confidence. This was the test that I needed.

Pickering did a lot of tough-talking to the press before the fight. He said that he would 'knock me out – fact'. He would 'beat me up'; he was 'walking out of that arena with the European title'. He boasted that I couldn't say that because I knew I wasn't good enough.

A lot of this sort of stuff goes on in professional boxing – building yourself up and making fun of your opponent. It's really all about selling tickets to the fight. The thing was, we didn't need any of this hard-man play-acting to sell the fight. It was already sold out. We had moved it to a bigger venue, the Point Depot, now known as the 3Arena, and the fans had got right behind it. So we didn't have to sell the event, unless they wanted to build an extension to the Point. What we had to do now was deliver a great fight, and I personally had to deliver a winning performance.

I didn't do too much talking at the press conferences. Pickering and his coach seemed to want to control the microphone, and that didn't bother me. I would happily do my talking in the ring.

Training had gone really well for the fight. We knew that we had to be prepared for a tough battle. Pickering was strong, and very unorthodox. He would talk to you in the ring, and try to get inside your head. This meant I would have to be very focused in there, and stick to the plan.

On the day of the fight, the Point Depot was heaving. The atmosphere and excitement, not just around the arena but around the town, was electric. I wasn't one for getting overly stressed or uptight before fights, but I could feel that this fight was different to all of my others. I had nerves – everyone does. As long as you can control them, nerves are a good thing. They show that you care about whatever it is you are doing.

The jab and hook to the body were going to be my main weapons. We knew that Pickering would keep switching stance to try to confuse me, but when he did, I was going to pound his body with hooks. Take a bit of life out of those thirty-year-old legs. Harry kept talking about the plan. Cementing it in my head. Box him, keep moving and, when you get a chance, attack that body.

Now it was getting close to fight time. The stadium manager came in to tell us to be ready for our ring walk.

Brian had played a blinder on this night. Pickering was the first to make the ring walk, and usually I would not be far behind. On this night, however, I wouldn't be as quick in making my entry. I was completely unaware of what was going on. I only found out after the fight that Brian had got a 'Bernard Dunne' double to come out on the balcony above the ring and look down on Pickering. Pickering must have been wondering what the hell I was doing up there. I'm sure the fans were just as curious to find out what I was doing when I should have been on my way to the ring.

Brian's plan was to keep Pickering standing and waiting for as long as possible. He achieved that. We made Pickering wait over thirteen minutes before I started to make my way in. One up team Dunne, and we hadn't even started throwing punches yet!

This was the night when I realised that something special was happening around boxing in Ireland. It was an amazing feeling to walk out in front of thousands of fans, all bubbling with excitement that big-time boxing was back in Ireland. They were anticipating a win, and an Irishman to be crowned European Champion. It was my job to deliver on that.

Our plan paid off as soon as the fight started. My jab was like a battering ram. Every time I threw it, he walked straight into it. Blood started to flow from the second round, and continued to do so for the rest of the fight. Pickering was a seasoned professional though, and he knew every trick in the book. He was holding me on one side with his left and clubbing me on the other side with his right. He was constantly trying to stand on my toes to stop me moving or, worse, to trip me up. He was hitting me with his head, his shoulders and his elbows.

We fought at a hectic pace, but I was in control. I was picking my shots well, and Pickering was getting more frustrated and desperate as the fight went on. In the second half of the fight, his corner kept shouting, 'He's getting tired, Esham,' and, 'You have him.'

I may be tired, I thought, *but there are only three rounds left.* I reckoned I could stay out of trouble that long.

I had that little monster inside my head well and truly under control, and I would keep it that way, apart from an incident in the tenth: I felt that Esham hit me after the bell, and I was having none of that. I swung back, and very quickly both of us were throwing punches. The referee jumped in to separate us and in doing so, pushed me to the ground. 'Come on!' Pickering shouted, but now the coaches from both corners had jumped in to make sure we stopped fighting – at least until the start of the next round!

Everyone in the arena was on their feet. Harry reminded me when we got back to the corner what the plan was: 'Keep boxing, Bernard ... These are the championship rounds now, so just keep moving ... He's got to come now, so be ready.' Sound advice, helping to calm me down and get me refocused. Harry was good at that. He knew me as a person and as a boxer. He understood what made me tick, and was able to use that to get the best out of me.

Getting me to stick to the plan now was important. We were ahead, and I just needed to see out the next two rounds. This was new ground for me. I had never gone this far in a fight before, so it was good to see that my fitness could handle it.

I got through the next two rounds with a constant voice shouting, 'be smart,' 'box,' and 'move,' and be smart, box and move was exactly what I did. Esham was trying to taunt me into fighting with him. 'Come on, you going to keep running?' he would say. I wasn't running; I was being clever, and I was also winning the round. The bell rang for the end of the twelfth.

I ran to the corner of the ring and jumped up on the ropes to celebrate. I didn't know the result yet, but I was fairly sure I had done enough to get the decision. Pickering also celebrated, more in hope than actually expecting to win. *There's only one way he is leaving Dublin tonight with that European belt,* I said to myself, *and that's by robbing it from my changing room.*

The ring was now packed with people – my family and friends, my boxing team and a whole lot of media people.

The referee, Massimo Barrovecchio, called both fighters to the centre of the ring. His shirt had been clean white at the start of the contest, but by now it was a nice shade of pink, with the splattering of blood that it had taken throughout the fight. It had been a real battle.

Mike Goodall, the ring announcer, started to deliver the decision. He read out the scores, and then said, 'And the new European Super-bantamweight Champion, Bernard Dunne!' I sank to my knees upon hearing my name called out. Our first major step had now been taken in the world of professional boxing. I was now ranked in the top ten boxers in the world in my weight division. This was exactly where I wanted to be, and at twenty-six, I was only starting to come into my peak years.

Harry and Brian had timed it perfectly, and now we had the belt to show for it.

'Christmas has come early, lads!' I shouted out to the crowd as I was being interviewed in the ring. Nobody was going home early that night. The arena was still packed as I finished up my TV interview in the ring.

As I was getting out of the ring and working my way back to my changing room, those words from legendary sports presenter Jimmy Magee rang out, all so true: 'Everyone wants to hug the winner.'

Chapter 10

Eighty-Six Seconds

We pulled into the house early the next morning, after spending the night in the Burlington hotel. Olive, Pamela's mam, had stayed home and minded baby Caoimhe while everyone else went to the fight. This was the reason I had made these choices, to train and push myself in boxing: my family. I tenderly picked up Caoimhe – not because she was a baby, but because both my hands were badly swollen. These are the realities of the job.

My plan was to take a break until after Christmas, and then get back at it. Becoming European Champion was bringing a little bit more public attention my way. I was being paraded on the pitch at Irish soccer matches, and walking out in front of the Hill in Croke Park. I even got invited on to the 'Late Late Show' for a chat.

This was all part of the business, building and promoting fights. In the middle of all of this came the little matter of making sure that my family were being rewarded financially for all of my hard work. Boxing for me was never about making money. I would have done it for free – I had been for years – but if there was an opportunity for me to make money doing something I loved doing, I was going to make the most of that opportunity.

Contract negotiations were tough, and not something I really enjoyed, but they were now a necessary part of my world. I had a figure in my head for my next fight that I would be happy with. I was, after all, topping the bill and selling out venues. I felt I should be paid accordingly. After several intense conversations with Brian, with Harry acting as peace-maker, we eventually settled on a figure. It was a lot closer to the figure I started with than the one I was first offered.

The business end of this game meant making cold decisions. I didn't mind what Brian or anyone else was making from my fights, so long as I was happy with what I was making. Our relationship would take a bit of a hit from this point on, but Brian and myself would continue to work together.

My first title defence would be against Yersin Zhailauov, from Kazakhstan, on 25 March 2007. It was a Sunday night. Sunday was an unusual night for boxing, but thankfully, it turned out to be a short night's work for me. Zhailauov made my low hands look like the Fort Knox of boxing defences. His hands were constantly low, and he paid for that in the third round.

We were out again quite soon afterwards, in June of the same year. This time I fought against an old amateur foe of mine, Reidar Walstad. He had beaten me at the European Championships in Belarus. He beat me well, in fairness to him. What had been planned as a long, tough tournament for me had ended after my first fight, and became a two-week sightseeing tour of Minsk instead.

Things had changed since that fight in 1998. I had changed. The one constant though was that Harry Hawkins would be working in my corner, as he had done at those championships. I did contemplate changing him for the night, but I don't believe in all that bad luck stuff.

At this point though, there was another fight being organised too. A name that was being mentioned constantly along with mine was Kiko Martinez. Kiko was a small, stocky Spaniard, and he was the number-one-ranked challenger for my belt. Our ideal venue, the Point Depot, would be closing at the end of August – if we didn't have the fight before then, there would be no suitable venue in Dublin to put it on.

First though, was Reidar Walstad, at the end of June. Harry told me I was crazy for fighting this close to the Kiko fight. 'We need to be focused on Kiko now, Bernard,' he would say. 'This guy needs one hundred percent of our attention.' I didn't mind who I was fighting though, or how often.

Walstad was a good guy, and we spoke a bit before the fight.

'Remember that fight in Belarus, where I beat you, Bernard?' he would say quite a bit.

'I was a kid back then, Reidar,' I would reply. 'Now I'm a man. Let's see what happens this time.'

Reidar was smaller than me, but quite blocky. We knew that he would be aggressive. He would try to walk in, with hands up, and unload when he got close enough to cause trouble.

I started off as normal, with the left jab. Reidar started to talk to me. 'Come on, let's fight,' he said as he waved me in with his fists. I kept sticking my left hand in his face, and hooking off it with both left and right hooks.

He got a nasty cut straight across his left eye, but for some reason it didn't bleed too badly. Walstad kept swinging away. He was game and came to fight, but I comfortably won, using my boxing ability and smarts. In the ring after the fight, Brian announced that the next fight would be against Kiko 'La Sensación' Martinez. Harry was still annoyed that we took on Walstad. Although I won comfortably, it was a tough twelve rounds of boxing that my body didn't need in the lead-up to Kiko.

Kiko was a little block of dynamite. He had a record of 16-0, with thirteen knockouts. With this fight coming up so quickly after Walstad, we didn't get much time to let the body rest. Harry came down to Dublin for the first week of camp, so I could have a little more time at home with my family. I was fully confident that I could handle Kiko and nullify his threat. Harry kept drilling into me to 'move, move, move'. Never be a still target for him to shoot at, Harry warned me. 'Box clever in the early rounds, Bernard,' he said. 'You will break him down in the second half of the fight.'

Yes, I'll box clever. This boy doesn't know what's coming, I told myself.

On the night, we met face-to-face in the centre of the ring for the referee's instructions. Back to my corner then, and Harry gave me his last bit of advice: 'Be alert and keep moving,' along with a gentle slap on the face.

Eighty-six seconds later, I was lying on the floor, with the referee, Terry O'Connor, standing over me.

What the hell just happened? I wondered.

I was brought over to my corner and sat on a stool.

'Is that it? Is it all over?' I asked. I began to protest, 'I'm alright.'

'Relax, Bernard. You're okay, son,' said Harry.

I was completely out of it. Kiko had caught me with a right hand over my jab, and it was like my body went into a state of shock from the shot. I knew what I wanted to do; I would tell my body what to do, but my body could not follow my instructions. I was moving in slow motion, while Kiko was moving like a steam train. He came forward relentlessly, until there was nothing left and I was finished.

The arena fell silent. The party atmosphere was no more. I was devastated. My pride was badly wounded. It is one thing to fail or to lose, but it is another thing to fail in the manner that I did – in front of the whole world. Okay, that may be an exaggeration, but that's how it felt at the time.

This was the first time I had ever been beaten on home soil. I went back to my changing room and just sat on the floor of the shower, thinking about what had just happened and where I could go from here. What went wrong? I asked myself. How could I have prepared better?

Physically, the fight took nothing out of me. I mean, it had only lasted eighty-six seconds. All of that training, to be knocked out in a minute-and-a-half.

I didn't sleep that night, and it wasn't because Pamela kept checking on me to make sure that I was okay. The doctors had told her to monitor me through the night. I was lying there, giving out to myself and wondering what was next. It seemed as if my twenty-two years of boxing had shrunk to those eighty-six seconds. I realised very quickly that I would have to stop thinking so negatively. I needed to move on, or I would never come back from this.

One defeat does not make you a bad fighter, whatever the press or certain people might say. I wasn't finished or washed up. Not in my mind anyway. I was as ready as I could have been for that fight; I just got beaten by a better man on the night, who executed his plan perfectly. I never took any notice when people were building me up, so I was most certainly not going to take any notice of them now, when they were trying to tear me down. As much as everyone wants to hug the winner, not many people want to stay on board what they presume to be a sinking ship. But other people's opinions of me were not my problem as far as I was concerned.

I trained the very next day after the fight. The journey was going to continue, and there was no time like the present to get started.

Chapter 11

The Road Back

On 14 February 2008, I sat down in an office in Dublin's Temple Bar with Harry and my solicitor, and Brian Peters and his solicitor, to sort out a deal to go forward with. I had negotiated all my own contracts up to this point in time, but I thought now that maybe it was better to bring in a professional to help with the drawing up of these agreements.

I really didn't enjoy this part of the business, but unfortunately it had to be done. And I wanted to be clear on where my career was going. It wasn't the most romantic way to spend Valentine's day, but I promised myself I would make it up to Pamela next year.

The venue for my comeback fight was going to be Breaffy House in County Mayo, a little different than what I was used to. My opponent was a tough, durable Venezuelan called Felix Machado. His best days were behind him, but he would still prove to be a tricky customer.

It was a strange night all round, and not only because it was my first fight in Ireland to be staged outside Dublin. I couldn't quite put my finger on it, but the audience seemed subdued or nervous somehow. I could sense it in the air. People kept asking me if I was alright – 'How are you feeling?' 'Are you relaxed?' They were doing my nut in to be honest. I had been knocked out; I hadn't lost my ability to fight!

I had made a couple of additions to my team since Kiko. 'You have achieved European level, Bernard, but if you really want to push on to the elite level, you're going to have to look at how you train and what people you have around you,' my Dad said. If I wanted to get to the top, we knew that we would need more than just boxing ability to get there. In all my years of boxing, I had never really done any weight lifting, and had relied on my skill to get me through my fights. Now I hired a strength and conditioning coach to add some steel to the boxing ability that I had.

A nutritionist was also brought on board. If I was going to be pushing my body to greater heights, I would need to be sure I was refuelling in the right way. Making 8st 10lbs was never easy for me either, and I hoped the nutritionist would also be able to help me with this.

This wasn't just the old Bernard Dunne, the boxer that the fans had seen in previous years. No, this was a new and improved version. One that had learned the art of keeping his hands up, for the most part! All thanks to Kiko.

Even still, the strange atmosphere walking into the ring that night did get to me. It kind of unnerved me. I was never like this. Why now? Surely Kiko hadn't affected me that much?

When we got to the ring, we realised that we had forgotten my gum shield, which was not the greatest of starts to the night. It was a basic mistake, but Harry was straight on to me to 'stay focused. We have a job to do here.'

Everybody seemed to hold their breath until the first punch was landed. It was me who landed it, and it seemed to put the crowd and myself at ease. This was how the fight was supposed to go. Machado was the perfect guy to get me back winning. He had a good record, was older than me and slower than me, and he liked to box. The perfect way to ease myself back in.

I ran out a comfortable winner on points. There was relief all round. The show was back on the road, and the crowd were happy to see me get through it.

A rematch was now firmly on my mind. I wanted to get back in the ring with Kiko as soon as possible. And Kiko wanted to get back in the ring with me too. Sure, why wouldn't he, after the easy night's work he had the last time we met? The problem in organising this match was that the two management teams wouldn't talk to each other. Brian flatly refused to do business with Kiko's team. It was hard to blame him really, after they had tried to muscle in on his show the last time.

In the gym, I really started to push myself. We had identified physical strength as my biggest weakness, and we wanted to change this. When I hit someone, we wanted them to know they had been hit. The Machado fight was a good example of the need to improve my power. Though I won the fight easily and was hitting him at will, I should have been able to put him away.

I was lifting weights that I had never done before, deadlifting, squatting and bench pressing. I won't lie and say that it was enjoyable, but I knew it was necessary, so I pushed through the pain. I think my strength and conditioning coach, Mikey McGurn, really enjoyed inflicting pain on people in the gym. My body would be crying, desperate to give up, but Mikey would force – sorry, I mean encourage – me to keep going, to get through two more sets than I ever thought I could do. It was not just physically challenging, but mentally too. I think that stood to me in the long run, knowing that I had really pushed myself to the limits.

We got an interesting offer in June of that year. Celestino Caballero, the World Champion, wanted to fight me. I'm sure this was after he watched me being destroyed by Kiko.

He was tall, and a big puncher at the weight. He had only been beaten twice in thirty-six fights – once by Jose Rojas, from Venezuela, and the other time by his countryman, Ricardo Cordoba.

Brian thought that this was the fight to take. 'You may never get this chance again, Bernard,' he said. But I felt it was too soon for me to fight him. 'I'm not ready,' I said, 'and I don't think the public are ready either.' We were still rebuilding. Firstly our strength, and then ours and the public's confidence that I was ready to fight for a world title.

Damian Marchiano was the next man I would face in the ring. Another confidence-builder, and another comfortable points victory. We then headed back out to Breaffy House, for what would nearly be the nightmare of all nightmares.

Christian Faccio, a rugged, walk-forward fighter, was very much in the mould of Kiko, but without that killer punch. I stuck to the plan this time though. I boxed, boxed and boxed some more, picking shots from distance and then mixing it up with some crunching body punches.

Round seven was very much like the six rounds that had gone before it. Faccio was chasing me around the ring, and I was popping him with some clean counter-punches.

I went to step inside, and he lunged forward just at the same time. Our heads clashed, and I got a sickening feeling as I saw the blood squirt out in front of me. I knew immediately that this wasn't like the normal cuts that I would pick up in fights. I was covered in blood within seconds, and my vision was starting to become blurred. The bell went to end the round, and the referee called the doctor over to check my injury.

They had a talk – the referee, the doctor and Harry – and I heard the words, 'He can't continue with that cut.' *Can't continue?* I started to worry, thinking that if they stopped the fight then that would mean I would lose.

'I'm grand, Harry,' I shout. 'Tell them I'm okay to fight. They have to let me go on, Harry. They can't do this!' I was in full-blown panic mode at this stage.

Harry just leaned in and said, 'It's okay, Bernard, it'll go to the scorecards, and you're going to win. Just relax.'

Harry was right. The fight had been stopped because of a cut caused by a clash of heads, so the result would be decided by the judges' scorecards at that stage of the fight.

Doctor Joe McKeever came into my changing room, where I was lying on the couch, nursing my wound. It was a nasty cut, right at the top of my forehead.

'Come into the bathroom for a second, Bernard, and I'll have a look at that,' said Joe. I sat down on the toilet seat, and Joe took hold of my head and cleaned off the cut to get a better look at it. As he pulled the skin, I winced a bit and pulled away.

'You'll be grand,' Joe said in a jolly manner. 'I'll throw a couple of stitches into it here, and you'll be like new.' He was always great at delivering bad news with a smile.

Now, I know that I am a boxer and I am supposed to be used to pain, and able for it, but with Joe running a needle and thread through the skin of my forehead, I was squealing like a little baby.

'Jaysus, Joe, are you nearly done?' I yelled at him.

'Just a couple more,' he said. 'I want to make sure it's good and tight, so it won't cause you problems in the future.'

The future? I thought. *I may not see it at this rate.*

The people outside the room must have thought Joe was trying to murder me, with the noise I was making. I survived, just about, but it was a nasty gash, which would need time to heal. More time for me to spend in the gym.

There was no real celebration at the result of this fight; just a feeling of relief. I still felt like I wasn't in full flow yet, but a win is a win.

More offers of fights were coming in. Brian wanted me to fight for a major belt now. England's Rendall Munroe held the European belt. We were trying to get him to come and fight me, but his team refused. They wanted us to go to them. But he was fighting in small halls with a couple of hundred fans, while we were filling large arenas. It made no financial sense to go there. Also, the British Boxing Board of Control wouldn't let me fight in their jurisdiction, because of the cyst on my brain.

Then an offer to fight for a world title arrived at our door. This was against the then-WBA World Champion, Ricardo Cordoba. Cordoba had beaten Celestino Caballero, who had offered me a shot at the world title the year before. It had been a risk to turn that one down, but I felt it was the right thing to do. I wasn't ready then, but I had rebuilt my confidence, and I was stronger now than ever before. I was turning twenty-nine. We felt that now was the right time to compete for the title.

Cordoba's team were looking to travel, to get some fights around Europe. Their plan was to keep their belt and make some easy money. They didn't see any of the fighters on this side of the Atlantic beating Cordoba. *Like taking candy from a baby,* they thought. Time would tell if I was up to the challenge.

Chapter 12

It's Ours, It's All Ours!

Holy Trinity Boxing Club in Belfast became like Fort Knox for my training camp leading up to this fight. Harry wanted 'no distractions'.

'Whatever contract you're sorting with Brian, get it done early,' he said. He didn't want me to be arguing about money on the week of the fight.

This was the opportunity I had been waiting for, so money was not going to be an issue for me. I had dreamed of this moment since I was a young child. The media no longer believed the dream, but that didn't bother me.

They were outside of my circle of trust.

They could write what they wanted in the paper, or say what they wanted on the TV or radio. It would have no impact on me one way or the other. Dad always said, 'Don't listen to what people outside have to say. What matters is what you think and what you believe.' I had a strict policy of not listening to any news reports that had anything to do with an upcoming fight. If you were inside the circle, and there were not many, then your opinion was valued and sought.

Two individuals most certainly inside this circle were my Dad and Harry. Both had great boxing brains. Both had nothing but my best interests at heart, and both told me that this was 'the perfect fight' for me. Cordoba was 'a tall, slick, fast, counter-punching southpaw', they told me, but 'he is made for you'. I had no problems fighting southpaws. Cordoba already had nine years' experience as a pro, even though he was still only twenty-five. He was obviously not just a good technical fighter – he was also a tough cookie if he was fighting as a pro from the age of sixteen.

Dad and Harry always studied my opponents and then fed me whatever information they felt was important, but they told me to study this guy a little more than I normally would. I watched videos of his fights, over and over again, examining every move he made. He liked to use his long reach. He would throw a big southpaw jab, followed by a straight left or an uppercut to the body. The more I watched, the more I could visualise how I was going to beat him. Growing up with all those southpaws in CIE was going to stand to me in this fight.

The fight was set for 21 March 2009. On that same day, Ireland would play Wales in a Six Nations rugby match, and if we won, we would win the grand slam. Dublin and Ireland was looking forward to one of the biggest sporting weekends in its history. I wasn't able to leave the hotel that day, as the streets were heaving with people, all fired up about the two events.

I watched the rugby in my room in the hotel. Watching the lads do their thing, winning the match and the grand slam, gave me an extra lift. I wanted more than anything to follow in their footsteps. We headed down to the venue around nine o'clock, through streets that were packed with people celebrating the rugby and heading into the stadium – the O2, previously known as the Point Depot and now the 3Arena. Whichever name you want to call it, the crowds were flooding in.

Security came out to meet us, guiding our car around to the side entrance. Cameras were ready and waiting for our arrival. As we stepped out of the car, we could just sense that this was different to anything that we had ever done before. People spotted me entering the venue and started singing 'There's only one Bernard Dunne, there's only one Bernard Dunne'. Up to the changing room we went and it was chill time.

I sat, thinking about all my preparations: The sparring partners that we had flown in from all over the world whose styles were like Cordoba's; round after round of giving shots, taking shots, getting into wars and then controlling that voice inside me so that I could get back to what I was good at – boxing. Staying in control would be pivotal in this fight. My mind had to be strong, and steady.

We did a light stretch, and then Harry began to wrap my hands. This took about thirty minutes, and then I started to loosen out and do some shadow boxing. My gloves were brought into the room. I slipped my hands inside, and my focus started to kick in. The room was now silent apart from Harry, repeating our fight mantra: 'Over his jab, Bernard.' *There he goes again, using my first name. This must be serious!*

'Stay on the outside, and come over his jab,' said Harry. 'You can outsmart and outbox this guy.' He was like a broken record.

We did some pads, and went over three or four of the combinations we had been working on. One of those was to flick out a jab, get low and then come up with a straight right hand, followed by a left hook.

There was a knock on the door. 'Show time,' came the voice. 'Get ready to make your walk.' This would be another first for me. I would be the one to wait in the ring, instead of making my opponent wait for me. That was going to be the Champ's honour tonight. I stood behind a big white sheet with drummers on either side of it, banging out the epic beat of 'O Fortuna' from *Carmina Burana*. The hairs on the back of my neck started to stand up as the crowd roared when they saw my shadow lit up behind the big sheet.

Cordoba popped out down at the end of the corridor behind me. We caught each other's eye, he yelled something to me in Spanish and I said something back to him. Neither of us could understand the other, but I think we both knew what we were talking about.

The sheet dropped as 'The Last of the Irish Rover' started to blare out on the sound system, and I was blown away by the sight in front of me. I have been in packed arenas before, but this was special. I am not sure that there were too many Panamanians in the crowd. This was my night. These were my people, and I was there to perform.

'Let's go to work,' shouted Harry, and I made my way through the crowd to the ring, surrounded by security. I passed my Dad, and we pumped fists. Yes, he knew that I was ready. As I made my way up the steps into the ring,

I stopped at the top step and raised my arm into the air. The roof nearly came off the arena.

Then Cordoba made his way casually to the ring, just as if he was out walking his dog. The hostility of the crowd did not faze him at all.

The anthems were played, and the announcer got his part out of the way. Now it was just Ricardo, referee Earle Hubert and myself in the ring. Earle gave us his last instructions: 'I spoke to you both in the changing rooms … I expect a good clean fight … Good luck to you both.'

There was no feeling each other out in this one. We were straight at it from the bell. Maybe Cordoba had watched the Kiko fight and thought, why waste time when he could just catch me early and blow me out of it in one round? The pace was relentless, with both of us having success when we attacked.

In the third round, I got backed up into one of the neutral corners. I got low, shot up with a right hand and followed with a left hook, just like we had practised. Boom, I landed with the hook and Cordoba went flying across the ring, crashing onto the floor. It was the perfect shot. For anyone who plays sport, you know when you have hit it on the button, be it soccer, Gaelic football or hurling – when you connect, like the way I connected, you know what way it is going to turn out. As soon as that left hook landed, I knew he was going down. I instantly thought, *That's it. It's over. I am Champion of the World.* I don't think in all my years of boxing, that I have ever landed a punch as cleanly.

The referee was counting away and the whole arena was celebrating and then, all of a sudden, Cordoba sat up and then stood up. I couldn't believe it. I thought, *Woah, what have I got to do to beat this guy?* The referee was still counting, but there were only seconds left in the round, so I didn't get the chance to finish the job and he made it through the round.

We came out for the fourth, and picked up where we had left off, both of us going at it. We clashed heads. 'Watch your heads!' shouted the referee, but I was cut. I had double vision from this point on. On seeing the blood, Cordoba got a burst of energy and went on the offensive.

I just wanted to get through the round without making the cut any worse, so I started to dance around the ring. I got back to the corner and Benny King, my cut man, fixed me up. 'It's nothing to worry about, Bernard,' he said, in his great Scottish accent.

Cordoba's new-found energy continued into the next round. He was straight out and attacking me from the bell. He had me under pressure, forcing me back. He managed to manoeuvre me into the corner, and unleashed a barrage of punches that put me down on my knees. I looked over to my corner to signal that I was okay.

I started to circle, trying to buy some time to regain my self-control, but Cordoba was all over me. We exchanged blows, and the next thing I remember was being on the floor. I was trying to stabilise myself by putting my hand on the floor, but I was all over the place. I looked up and I saw my Mum, but she wasn't looking at me. She had her head buried in my Dad's chest, and I was thinking, 'What's wrong with my Mum?' It was only then that I realised I was on the floor and in a fight.

I then had a strange experience. Now, you may think this sounds a little crazy, or even that I am a little crazy, but in that moment I actually started to have a conversation with myself. I had come out of my body, and I was talking down to myself. We had a chat: What was next? If I stayed down, that was it, it was all over. People would say, 'Great effort, well done, but hard luck. What will you do now, now that you're finished with boxing?' What seemed like a twenty-minute conversation was, in reality, only three or maybe four seconds.

I came back to the present moment, inside the ring with Harry shouting at me, 'Get up! Get on your feet!' I stood up, still really in a daze, but I told the referee that I was fine and I wanted to go on. He let the fight continue, and there was still plenty of time left in the round for Cordoba to finish the job. He sensed victory, and was straight in for the kill. Backing me up onto the ropes, he started unloading punches, hitting me with everything he had. He was swinging away, but I blocked him with my new-found defence and high guard.

The clock was ticking away slowly, and the referee was ready to jump in to separate us. *Ding ding!* came the bell, and Earle jumped right in between us and screamed, 'STOP!' I had just unleashed a right hook, right on the bell, and it brushed right past Earle. An inch closer and he would have caught it clean on the chin. I tapped him on the backside as I went past and said, 'Wow, nearly got you there!' He smiled, and I headed back to my corner.

I sat down on the stool, and Harry was amazed at how clear my eyes were. He expected me to be bleary-eyed, but I was focused, looking straight at him.

'Okay, that's just one round you lost,' he said. In our plan, we had broken the fight down into twelve individual fights. Win seven out of twelve and I would be World Champion. So this was just one of those twelve that I had lost. It was a good way for us to keep it all in perspective.

'Okay, so that's his round,' Harry continued. 'Careful now; get back behind your jab. Let's not give him any free shots.'

I stood up at the start of the sixth, and raised my arm in the air in a sign of defiance. 'You can hit me all you want,

Ricardo, but I am coming back for more,' was the message I wanted to give out. I don't think the crowd could believe I was coming back out, and I could see on Cordoba's face that he really couldn't believe it.

The bell rang, and the roar from the crowd was deafening. Instead of retreating, as most would do when they have been hurt, I walked right out and held my ground. I felt that if I ran, Cordoba would give chase and try to corner me and start unloading his shots again. This way, I was controlling the centre of the ring and making Cordoba think.

I was able to keep him off me, and I landed some nice shots. The next four rounds were back and forth, with both of us landing some good clean punches to head and body, causing some damage to each other.

When the bell rang to start the tenth round, Cordoba ran out of his corner, and he threw as many punches in that round as he had thrown in the entire fight up to then. He either felt that I was tiring, or that he was losing on points, but whatever the reason for it, he pushed me right to the brink in that round.

I got through it, and Harry said to me in the corner, 'Right, son, championship rounds now. Let's finish big. Remember, keep compact and always finish with that big left hook.'

I started the eleventh round trying to put Cordoba on the back foot, but he held his ground. I caught him with a clean right hand, but it probably caused me as much pain as it did him, sending shock waves the whole way up my arm. The pain soon disappeared though, as Cordoba's legs started to wobble and he fell back towards the ropes. I gave chase this time, and landed a combination that sent Ricardo tumbling to the floor.

He looked hurt now. The whole arena was on its feet. But Cordoba had great heart. He would not give in as long as there was any energy left in those legs of his.

He pulled himself up by the ropes, and the referee let the fight continue. I walked out to meet him in the centre of the ring. I connected with a left hook, and he hit the floor again. I looked to my corner, and Harry was yelling, 'Get after him, don't let him off!'

Cordoba, like a true warrior and champion, got himself back to his feet, and the referee once again let us go at it. I went out to close him down, and let off a combination, but I fell in and Cordoba grabbed hold and smothered my shots.

Harry was going crazy in the corner at this stage, slapping the canvas and screaming 'Get off him! Let your hands go!' He could see that this was my chance, and that time was running out. I started to jab and stalk Cordoba from a safe distance, like a lion stalks his prey. I backed him into his corner and, as he tried to get out of it, I crouched low and then sprang up with that right hand and left hook combination.

With 2.59 on the clock in the eleventh round, Ricardo Cordoba hit the canvas for the third and final time. I turned in ecstasy and fell to the floor myself in celebration. The referee waved the fight over, and Bernard Dunne had just become Champion of the World!

All of the choices that I and those around me had made – like not eating Easter eggs as a kid, my Grandad bringing me to the club every Sunday morning, my Dad getting picked up off the kitchen floor by Mammy Dunne after sparring, leaving my home and my family for weeks at a time for training camp – everything that Pamela, my family, my friends and my team had put into it – it had all led up to this moment.

Champion of the World. It was incredible. Two years previously, I was finished, washed up. The dream was over in the eyes of many people, after I had been knocked out in eighty-six seconds by Kiko Martinez. Yet here I was, after a battle that would be voted the fight of the year, the new WBA Champion of the World.

Between the rugby grand slam earlier that day and then my victory, this day would be remembered by many an Irish man and woman as one of the greatest days in Irish sporting history. I am extremely proud to be a part of that memory, and I thank Kiko Martinez for helping me to achieve it.

Without Kiko knocking me out and beating me like he did, I would never have learned a lot of hard lessons. I had had to look at myself, at my training methods and my team, and make the changes that were needed to achieve the ultimate goal of becoming World Champion.

I believe that everything happens for a reason, be it good or bad; you just need to be sure that you learn from it when it doesn't go your way. I didn't see it at the time, but Kiko was a blessing in disguise.

Marty Morrissey climbed into the ring and asked, 'How does it feel to be Champion of the World?'

'It's ours, it's all ours!' I roared in triumph.

Chapter 13

The End of the First Chapter

My world had been changed when I won that fight.
Not just from the point of view of being spotted and
recognised everywhere I went, but also in my own
thoughts, in what I wanted. I was enjoying a well-earned
break, and spending some quality time with my family.
The belt, after doing the rounds of several TV shows
and dinner events, spent most of its time in the boot of
my car. It was strange. I had become what I had always
dreamed of becoming, but the belt didn't really mean a
whole lot to me.

Maybe this was because, as much as things had changed in my life, they had also stayed the same. Fight negotiations were a pain, as money and contracts were again raising their heads as problems, and Pat Magee, who was Kiko's promoter, was becoming an even bigger one. He again wanted to be a part of what we were doing. He may have thought that he was doing right, but it was all making my boxing life more complicated and harder to bear by the day.

Harry and I wanted a voluntary defence, but Brian had failed to get an agreement from Thai boxer Poonsawat Kratingdaenggym and his team that would allow us to have one. Pat Magee had stuck his nose into all of this and signed an agreement with Poonsawat, just like he had done with Kiko. All of this was distracting me from what I really should have been concentrating on.

Money and control were the issues that were preventing Brian and Pat from sitting down together and thrashing out a deal. Each was as bad as the other, as far as I was concerned. It's funny, as my biggest challenges should have been in the ring.

It got to the stage where I didn't care who I fought; I just wanted something finalised and signed. I was tired of all the talk. Then, even when the fight was all agreed, the problems still didn't go away. Two weeks before it was supposed to happen, news broke that Pat Magee was threatening to stop the fight from going ahead, after some kind of disagreement between him and the Thai camp.

Fight night, 26 September, finally arrived. I was as ready as I was going to be. Poonsawat looked like a mini tank in the ring, but I was the Champion, and I had grown a lot over the past few years, physically and mentally. This fight would challenge me on both fronts.

Poonsawat came out very aggressively from the very first bell. He was right in my face, in that style that I really don't like. It was like Kiko part two, but I had learned a wee bit since that night, which helped me to avoid Poonsawat's big bombs.

His power, when he did hit me, was like nothing I had ever felt before. Every time he hit me, I winced.

The first two rounds went by, and I had won them by keeping my distance and using my hand speed and combinations to keep him off me. But I was starting to think to myself, *I can't do this for twelve rounds.* I made a decision to attack him going into the third round. *I'm going to hit him with all that I've got while I'm still strong*, I told myself. I'll discourage him from just walking forward.

I walked out into the centre of the ring at the start of the third, and tried to stand my ground, but Poonsawat was soon forcing me back. I landed a big right hand, followed by a left hook, and he didn't even blink. I tried to trade blows with him, but he was like granite – he just wouldn't budge. Those clubbing right hands and left hooks to the body and head were really starting to have an effect on me.

A flash of light came from somewhere and I found myself lying on the floor. That flash of light was the impact of a thunderous right hand from Poonsawat. It was just like in a cartoon, when a character gets hit with a frying pan or something, and they start to see tweety birds. Me, I saw flashes of light. I would see that flash of light another two times before the referee stepped in and stopped the fight, with me laying on my back looking up at the ceiling of the arena.

And just like that, my belt had been taken away. What had been so incredibly hard and had taken so long for me to win, was just whipped away in a flash. A stool was brought into the ring. I was placed sitting up on it, and an oxygen mask was put on my face. I looked around me at a circle of worried faces. Professor Jack Phillips was in the ring, along with Dr Joe McKeever, and they were checking me out.

Jack said later that the sound of the punches I was taking was frightening. He told me that the shots Poonsawat was catching me with sounded like thunder claps. Jack was hearing the thunder, and I was seeing the flashes of light – Poonsawat really did bring a storm with him when he stepped into that ring.

That's life inside a boxing ring. There are only two of you in there, and only one can come out on top. This time it wasn't me. I hate losing, but I was beaten by a better man. I can accept that. There wasn't much more I could have done in that fight. Kiko never hurt me when he beat me in eighty-six seconds, and I would have loved to fight him again, as I felt I could have beaten him in a rematch.

Poonsawat though, he physically hurt me with every shot he caught me with. I wouldn't have been in the same rush to fight him again.

I went up to my changing room, and the crowd left and went home. It was just me, Harry and my family. I was put under observation by the doctors for the night, but it was just a precaution.

When I went home the next day, the kids, in their magical way, made me feel a whole lot better about life. They didn't care that their Daddy had just been beaten, and had lost his world title. They just saw Daddy and smiled. They really do help you forget what you think are problems.

It was time to rest, to take a break. Maybe even a longer break than was expected. After a couple of weeks of peace and rest, I started to think about my future. *Do I really want this anymore?* I asked myself. *Am I willing to go through all of that again?* I was questioning whether boxing would be a part of my future anymore, which was a completely new experience for me. Even after being knocked out by Kiko, I never once thought about stepping away from the sport.

The fact was, boxing was starting to feel like a chore, like something I no longer wanted to do. November came, and by now my mind was made up. I didn't want it anymore. The hardship of boxing alone as a sport is tough to deal with. But when you add on top of that the pressure of dealing with management and promotional issues leading into fights, it can really wear you out. The whole experience was beginning to turn sour for me.

I didn't want to remember boxing as something I didn't like, so I decided that I would retire. I told no one except for my wife. I eventually told my family and Harry, around Christmas time, but I told them that I didn't want anyone outside the circle to know. I just wanted to see how it felt when I told someone; I wasn't sure how I would deal with other people knowing that I was going to retire. Dad was his usual self, just like when I was a kid: 'If you want to box, son, box; if you don't, don't.' A very straightforward man, my Dad, but he always knew the right thing to say to me.

After a couple of weeks, nothing had changed in my mind, so we announced it to the public on 19 February 2010.

That chapter of my life was now over. I wasn't sure what the next few pages would read like.

For three months, life was good. I was eating what I wanted, and doing what I wanted. Simple things like bringing the kids to school and picking them up was such a pleasure. Going out for dinner or a drink though soon became boring for me. I wasn't doing anything with myself, which didn't help.

One night, I was watching some boxing on TV. In fact, it was a European title fight in my old weight division, and I started thinking, 'I could beat both of these guys ... In a couple of months, I could be European Champion ... Maybe retiring was the wrong decision ...'

I called Pamela into the room, and told her how I had been feeling over the last few weeks, and what I was now thinking. As we all now know, I never went back to boxing, so that tells you exactly what Pamela thought of the idea. It wasn't put across to me in the politest of terms, so I won't repeat what she said here. Really, it was probably just a passing daydream.

The real issue was that I wasn't doing anything useful with all of my new spare time. I was used to always knowing what I was doing, 24/7, 365 days of the year. Now, all of a sudden, I had all this time on my hands, and I was doing nothing with it. I had left behind the one thing I was good at, and I began to feel that I had no other skill or talent. I had way too much time to think to myself.

One morning, I was up with the wise old man, Brendan Dunne. I told him how I was feeling, and what I was thinking. He said, 'Son, just try whatever it is that interests you, or that you think you might like to do, and see what happens. What's the worst thing that can happen? You could try something and find that you don't like it. Well, grand, at least then you will know. But, son, you could also try something and find out that you enjoy it – or, better still, you could find out that you are actually good at it.' Simple advice as always from Dad, and that is exactly what I did.

I have tried plenty of things since that day. Some worked and some didn't, but at least now I was occupying my time

and not thinking about boxing. In the nine years that I
have now been retired, I have learned the Irish language;
I have hosted my own TV and radio shows; and I have
challenged the youth unemployment problem with
Microsoft – we got 10,000 eighteen-to-twenty-five-year-
olds off the live register and engaged or reengaged with
education. I have written two books and a TV show; and
I have been involved with the Dublin senior football team
now for six years.

My life has recently gone full-circle, and I am back
involved in boxing, as the High-Performance Director of
Irish Boxing. From the kid who at five years of age couldn't
reach the bag, dreaming of fighting on the biggest stages, I
am now leading the Irish national boxing team.

I loved my time boxing, and I got out at the right time,
so that my love for it would not fade. My life is very
different now and, if I am to be honest, so much more
fulfilling. I have never been afraid to challenge myself,
and my current role as High-Performance Director is
challenging in many ways.

I believe that if you want to be something or if you want to do something, then you should try to take that chance, try to achieve whatever it is you dream of. Who knows where it could bring you? The second chapter of my life is just beginning, and I am looking forward to the challenges it will bring.

Slán go fóill mo chairde.